W0246633

PUFFIN BOOKS

FULL ON FASHIONISTA!

Born in Mumbai, Sonja has lived in Africa, Middle East and USA. Copywriter, columnist and novelist, she co-hosted and successfully organized the Pune International Literary Festival 2013.

Sonja currently resides in Pune, India with her three rambunctious children, a golf-crazy husband, Cheetos and OJ, the frisky family cats, and madcap friends, always hoping to travel the world through her stories.

She truly believes that a sense of humour makes life sparkle . . . and that a bit of dreaming can make magic happen! To know more about her upcoming work, do visit her author page on Facebook or at www.sonjachandrachud.com

Also in Puffin by Sonja Chandrachud

Potion of Eternity

Pearls of Wisdom

DOA Detective Files: Trouble at the Taj

DOA Detective Files: The Revenge of the Pharaoh

FULL ON FASHIONISTA!

Sonja Chandrachud

PUFFIN BOOKS
An imprint of Penguin Random House

PUFFIN BOOKS

USA | Canada | UK | Ireland | Australia
New Zealand | India | South Africa | China | Singapore

Puffin Books is part of the Penguin Random House group of companies
whose addresses can be found at global.penguinrandomhouse.com

Published by Penguin Random House India Pvt. Ltd
4th Floor, Capital Tower 1, MG Road,
Gurugram 122 002, Haryana, India

Penguin
Random House
India

First published in Puffin by Penguin Books India 2014

ISBN 9780143333302

Typeset in Perpetua Std by Eleven Arts, Delhi
Printed at Repro India Limited

www.penguin.co.in

MIX
Paper from
responsible sources
FSC® C047271

This is a legitimate digitally printed version of the book and therefore might not
have certain extra finishing on the cover.

CONTENTS

CONTENTS

ACKNOWLEDGEMENTS

Full On Fashionista is dedicated to all the wild, wacky and wonderful fashionistas in my life.

My mother who taught me all about timeless style and elegance.

Seemaa Singh, my dearest friend and now a celebrated fashion designer, who turned her dream into reality.

My crazy gym buddies, kudos for celebrating fashion and our friendship very seriously☺

Divia Thani, the elegant, soft-spoken editor of *Conde Nast Traveller,* who was kind enough to put me in touch with the very gracious Rituparna Som, Managing Editor of *Grazia.* Thank you, lovely ladies, for taking the time off your busy schedules and answering all my queries.

Sohini Mitra, my most wonderful editor, who insisted that I drop everything else and write this funky fashion story. 'It's so you,' she had rightly said.

Mimi Basu, the sweet yet ruthless editor, who made sure every word I wrote in this story is a runaway success.

Pia Hazarika, the immensely talented illustrator, behind the funky book cover.

And most of all my dahling diva girls Rhea, Paloma and Cheetos who teach me a thing or two about fashion and attitude every single day!

To quote the iconic fashion guru Karl Lagerfeld, **'Everyone has to invent his or her own thing.'**

And so, whether fashionista or not, I hope you enjoy this story and chase your dreams.

Full On.

OMG! (OH MY GAWD!)

'Geeeetaaanjaaliii . . . . .!!! Are you ready? We're leaving in five minutes!! God that child, I tell you Anand! When will she ever learn? You've spoilt her rotten.'

That, if you guys haven't already figured it out, is my dearest mother. But here's the catch. I don't have an ordinary, plump, cuddly-wuddly, cootchie-cooing, aloo paratha-stuffing, motherly mom like the rest of the teenagers of India. My mother happens to be none other than—hold your breaths—the celebrity actress Kajol Kulkarni! Slim, svelte, sexy, stunning . . . red carpet walking-talking SUPERSTAR.

'Just relax, Kajol darling. Why don't we go ahead and she'll come along with Sulu. Here, have a glass of wine.'

That's my Dad. Anand Kulkarni. Cool Karni is what everyone calls him. Nothing ruffles Dad. Yup, not even Mom's temper tantrums get under his skin. He's like James Bond: cool, calm, collected but yes, a bit too crazy when it comes to staying fit. 5 a.m. jogs, soccer practice, golf, all artfully scheduled in between his many business deals. I secretly wonder if he really is all that crazy about exercising or if it's a convenient excuse to stay away from Mom's melodramas . . .

'That's a great idea, Anand. I'll get Angie to come with me and you take Kajol out of here before she ruins her make-up with her frowns.'

That's Sulu, Sulochana Saxena, Mom's outrageous mother, and my adorable grandmother who hates my name as much as I do. So she changed it. And now everyone calls me Angie. 'Sounds hip and chic, like a Londoner,' says Sulu, her eyes twinkling. My grandma's quite the traveller. Been all over the world with three husbands, one dead and two divorced; and boy can she still make heads turn with her aristocratic looks, her silver hair, her chain-smoking, whiskey drinking and other such flamboyant habits.

My cell rings.

'Hey Angie, have a great time. Let's meet tomorrow, I'll help you with algebra, and yes, we'll go over the Pythagoras's theorem again and the sums we revised last week.'

That's Venky, my almost six foot, skinny, spectacled, nerdy 200 IQ neighbourhood school friend and homework guru. His grades are sky-high, he plays the piano almost like Mozart, teachers adore him, never mind the fact that Venky needs a complete wardrobe makeover twice over every single morning to make sure he doesn't embarrass me at school! I make a mental note to give Venky hell for spilling my mid-term grades to Mom.

Another call's coming in.

'Hey ya, gurl!! . . . Have a great time and for god's sake, don't freak your mom out. Wear whatever she's got for you . . . even though it's probably not your type. Remember today is *her* special evening.'

That's Sam. Sampurna Banerjee, my BF since middle school, and the one I rescued from school bullies. She knows all, and I mean knows ALL my secrets, and has sworn to take them to her grave. Sam's a plump, five-foot foodie, highly intuitive and so bloody stubborn about silly things that very often I want to strangle her. She's so unlike her globetrotting spa owner parents swishing around in their khadi silks, spouting Gibran. In fact, she doesn't even look like them!

'C ya later, Venky,' I disconnect. 'Ya, okay, Sam. I'll wear her stuff. Gotta get off now and shower; just got back from MMA class (that's Mixed Martial Arts for the uninitiated); kicked some serious butt! Bye! Gimme half an hour, okay; Grandma?'

That's me. Geetanjali 'Angie' Kulkarni, wishing I had a more exotic, intriguing name like Paloma, Rhea, Tamara, Nikki, Coco. Wishing I was a thinner, fairer and sassier teenager. Would have made school life sooo much more interesting at Royale International instead of having to lurk around the cafeteria like a vampire hoping that someday, someone will love the real me . . . I stare in utter desperation at the hideous fuchsia-pink ethnic outfit I must wear tonight.

I've tried every plea, trick and threat during the fittings to let Mom know I utterly hate that dratted outfit, but she was ridiculously adamant, refusing to understand my point of view!

'Angie dahling, don't be so stubborn, this is the Movie Mania Awards, India's most prestigious film awards ceremony, you know. Can't walk in there wearing something casual and chalta hai!'

'But last year Keya Kapur turned up . . .'

'Yes and it was a scandal, a leading actress landing up in a torn ganji and jeans trying desperately to look hip! Puhleez, spare me!' Mom's snorted derisively. 'And remember how the press massacred her? Poor girl, she still hasn't managed to get them off her back, however hard she tries.'

'I like Keya's style, it's so original. Why can't I wear my rhinestone studded jeans and . . .'

'Angie, that's enough, you'll wear what I've decided.'

But Mom, I've had enough, am tired of being pushed around. I'm not going to be found dead in that thing . . . I have rights—fashion rights, even if I'm just a teenager. I'm going to follow my heart just like Selena Gomez! I toss away the pink chiffon monstrosity, pump up David Guetta, raid my secret wardrobe (yup I have one tucked away from prying eyes), and decide to take a shot at wearing my own creation.

Now please note that this is a very brave and foolish thing to do when one has just thirty minutes to defy parents and decide on the ultimate showstopper. While I frantically tear through all my funky ensembles wondering which one will fit the bill tonight, the clock's ticking and I still have to grab a shower. Ten minutes later I've entered extreme panic zone. How can I, Angie Kulkarni, have nothing to wear? That's not possible! Wait a minute . . . There it is. I delve excitedly into the pile and pull out the Lady Gaga inspired neon-green ruffled dress I've designed using one of Mom's discarded chiffon saris—my latest, craziest fashion creation. This will be the perfect showstopper for tonight.

* * *

'Surprise . . . What do you think Sulu? Punk rock is the look this season,' I step out, my heart hammering wildly.

The fact that my grandma's jaw has dropped to the ground, her cigarette now dangling dangerously on her lips, doesn't strike me as worrisome. On the contrary, I do believe that she's stumped, simply amazed and astounded at my creativity. I proudly strut down an imaginary catwalk. This design is my current favourite; it inspired me all night before the maths exam, keeping me awake till dawn, and ended with me . . . erm . . . flunking the exam.

'It's . . . uh . . . ummm . . . quite a strong fashion statement, I must say, Angie. Let's hope your mom doesn't have a heart attack. Maybe tonight you should just stick with what she's got for you,' Sulu tries to sweet-talk me.

'Well, I'm not wearing that horrid thing Mom's got me. It's either this or I ain't coming!' I have my mother's genes all right, and Sulu knows better than to cross paths at this point; she gives in to my combat boots and all!

* * *

Walking in late is such a diva thingee, isn't it? And it's even sweeter when people gasp and stare at you as you sashay your way down the aisle to the front row, catching the flashbulbs of the paparazzi. The sudden hum of voices chattering excitedly in my wake excites me. I've just made a fashion statement with the eye-popping, neon-green ruffled dress over black fishnet stockings, ending in the knee-high boots. Yoohoo!

My heart's pounding and I sit down next to Dad, who strangely jumps out of his skin when he notices me. It's like he's seen a ghost. I smile at him; he shrinks deeper into his seat as if trying to melt away. What's with him? I wonder, and turn my attention to the dancers on stage, ignoring the rather frantic gesturing that's taking place between Dad and Sulu. Just then, Mom slips into her seat next to Dad across the aisle; pity she missed my entry. She looks spectacular as always, exquisitely regal in Suzanne Singh's Mughal ensemble but a bit *too* dolled-up desi for my liking. Methinks she looks lovelier in jeans and a T. I try and catch her attention but she is busy making small talk with her director Siddharth Samarth and ignoring her rivals, making sure the cameramen catch her best angles. The dancers exit and the over-gelled male anchor saunters back onstage, followed by a size zero Barbie lookalike counterpart.

Over-gelled dude drawls in a fake American accent.

'I'm Kevin and this is Cheryl, your co-hosts for this year's Movie Mania Awards, the country's most awaited, prestigious and spectacular film awards that honour the very best in Indian cinema. And now, for one of the most coveted Movie Mania Awards—the Best Actress . . .' He pauses dramatically. A thunderous roll of ghastly music adds to the rising tension. I clasp Dad's hands and pray. Please let Mom win! A hush descends as Cheryl, the Barbie lookalike, opens the envelope. Another loud roll of drums. Dad's grip tightens on my fingers.

'Ladies and gentlemen, tonight's winner is none other than . . . a multitalented actress with over ten critically acclaimed movies to her name; a performer whose career has stood the test of time; an extraordinary artiste who has been nominated to this year's Academy Awards, the Oscars . . . Ladies and gentlemen, please put your hands together for none other than Kajol Kulkarni, the lead actress in the film *Mysterious Maharani*!'

The crowd goes absolutely wild, clapping, whistling, cheering, flashbulbs popping every second! The applause is beyond deafening. Thrilled to bits, Dad forgets his corporate stiff upper-lip etiquette, he jumps up and scoops Mom in his arms, his eyes shining with pride. Oblivious of the crowd, he whispers something in her ear; she blushes and hugs him back.

'You totally rock Mom!' I yell, trying to get her attention, but am drowned out by another fresh bout of hysterical applause as Mom now gracefully glides up to the stage. I can't stop cheering. Sulu can't stop clapping and Dad, well, he's on top of the world right now, grinning from ear to ear. Mom takes the mike, smiling, waving ever so elegantly, as she waits for the audience to settle down.

'My dear fellow artistes, thank you all so very much for this prestigious award and for your constant faith, support and belief in me over the past many years.' Mom's honeyed tones waft over the audience but her eyes glitter as she slowly scans the crowd. Oops, I know that look. Mom is getting ready to launch into one of her legendary tantrums. Dad begins fidgeting in his seat, gearing up to whisk her away before things get out of hand.

'Oh, not now Kajol. Just let it go and enjoy your moment,' Sulu mutters under her breath.

'The road to success is never easy; hard work and talent go hand in hand when you dream of being a superstar. People have belittled my success by implying that I simply got *lucky*. So yes my dear friends . . . I got lucky, very lucky every single time. Ten times,' She pauses, dropping her voice to let her words sink in. 'Ten lucky times that my movies were box office hits?' she raises an eyebrow mockingly. 'And now I'm really *lucky* to represent Bollywood at none other than the Academy Awards, the Oscars.'

Nervous laughter breaks out, a few clap but her rivals sit petrified in their seats, watching Mom's every move.

'I guess with this kind of phenomenal luck on my side, I promise you there are miles to go before I sleep . . .'

There it was—the classy Robert Frost quote, a hidden warning to her critics that Kajol Kulkarni was still queen bee. Then, just as unpredictably, Mom's dark mood changes, the sneer leaves her voice and her eyes sparkle with joy once again.

'So, once again a huge thank you to everyone, my fans and directors. But most of all, my family who inspires and supports me every step of the way.'

Mom gets a standing ovation. Dad and Sulu look visibly relieved.

'Congratulations, Kajolji! We all look forward to your success at the Oscars. And I believe that there's one very special person in the audience tonight, your one and only child, your daughter Geetanjali . . . .' Cheryl whispers something and Mom nods in agreement. 'Would the lovely Ms Geetanjali Kulkarni please join us on stage so that we can meet, shall I say, the next superstar?'

A spotlight finds me. Excited, I begin to rise out of my seat, but Dad refuses to let go of my hand; he keeps pulling me down. He's saying something frantically shaking his head, but the roar of applause is too loud and I cannot hear him. I pull my hand out of his grip, stand up and head for Mom, utterly oblivious of the sudden deafening silence that has now engulfed the room.

'Are you all right?' I ask, for Mom has suddenly turned this putrid shade of yellow, making her make-up stand out in blotches. She looks like she's about to faint.

'What the hell are you *wearing*?' Mom hisses, her fingernails burying themselves deep into my skin, making me gasp out in pain. Her lips smile but her eyes are sharp daggers of hate, and it's then I realize that I'm in really serious trouble. 'Why didn't you wear the Suzanne Singh I got you?'

'Come on everyone, let's give a huge round of applause to the young Geetanjali Kulkarni,' Cheryl pounces on me with a gigantic smirk on her face as she eyes me up and down. 'And what *exactly* are you wearing Geetanjali? It's sooo different . . . hain na Kevin?'

The silence in the room has turned into a ripple of sniggers that is quickly gathering into a storm of derisive laughter and heading straight our way.

'It's punk rock fashion, you know, like the kind singer Avril Lavigne wears . . . Versace, John Galliano are well known for this trend,' I mumble, words rushing out frantically. 'This outfit is actually my own design . . .' I trail off as a thick knot of fear wells up in the pit of my stomach. What's going on? I wonder, terrified. What have I done? Flashbulbs are popping away in my face, blinding me.

'Ramona Vakil of the Starry News Channel has a question for Kajolji.' Oh dear god! It's none other than Ramona Vakil, the mother of Nikita, my nemesis at school. Ramona's the anchor for the popular Bollywood gossip channel and she's right up front. Like mother, like daughter. I just know she's going to drum up trouble.

'Kajolji, you are one of India's best dressed women, so where has your daughter inherited *this* great sense of fashion from?' Ramona's sharp nasal voice cuts through, the sarcasm unmistakable. 'You know, the in-your-face kinda street clothes these days . . . the wannabe fashionista kinds?'

I sense rather than see Mom stiffen up angrily and instinctively know that poor Cheryl's in really deep trouble for highlighting my somewhat radical wardrobe and setting the media on my tail.

'Geetanjali is a teenager and you know how teenagers are, Ms Vakil, always trying to be different by experimenting with their hair, clothes and whatnots . . .' Mom's voice is icy and controlled. Her fingers dig deeper into my arm as she steadies her rage trying to salvage the unsavoury situation. She moves closer to Cheryl, smiles, and stretches her other arm out as if to embrace her. Then she bends in ever so slightly, as I hear the threat that zips Cheryl up. *'One more question from the media about her dress and I'll rip your career to shreds.'*

Cheryl pales and hurriedly turns to the audience.

'Well, am sure that answers your question, Ramona. And, of course, we all love the funky way teenagers dress nowadays. And it's so amazing that you've designed this yourself Geetanjali . . .' Cheryl rambles on terrified. 'Ladies and gentlemen, please put your hands together for the lovely mother and daughter duo, Kajol and Geetanjali Kulkarni. We wish them all the very best!'

Two gorgeous bouquets appear out of the wings. Mom accepts, smiles and makes her way off the stage, dragging me into the waiting arms of a very worried-looking Sulu, who wastes no time in packing me off home before Mom explodes right there and then.

2

SOS (HELP!)

Waiting for a time bomb to go off is an extremely excruciating feeling especially when you're the one who's planted it.

I stay up all night for Mom to get home and royally bring the roof down, thrash it out with me like she always does, but she's nowhere to be seen. Somehow I get through the night, drifting between wanting to apologize to Mom versus standing up for myself.

I wake up to the smell of sizzling butter. My stomach rumbles; haven't eaten anything last night and boy am I starving! I step out of my room, go down the staircase and head for the kitchen and my heart lurches . . . There she is at the breakfast table, sipping her green tea, reading the papers, not a hair out of place. In fact a bit too calm and quiet for my liking. My mouth goes dry.

'Good morning, Mommy!' I chirp. She doesn't even glance my way. I'm suddenly overcome with remorse. 'Am so sorry about last night; it's just that . . . I simply couldn't wear that outfit you got me. It's really beautiful, it honestly is, but it's somehow not *me*!' I just blurt it out before Sulu can shut me up.

Mom looks up, her eyes glinting dangerously behind her spectacles, her mouth twisted in a bitter curl. I ready myself for the explosion.

'How could you do this to me, Geetanjali? How *could* you?' Her voice is cold, flat and unforgiving. 'Everyone's laughing at you, at me . . . for god's sake!'

Mom's always been my fashion idol. When she was younger and just starting out, her clothes would be funkier, bolder. Even her saris were different: bright, shiny, and sparkly, like a parakeet, and her blouses, daring and amazing. She even wore a bikini in a movie and didn't think twice about that!! So why was she, of all people, going nuts over my fashion experiment?

'Just let it go, Kajol,' Sulu warns. She knows her daughter's anger well. 'Angie's a child and her outfit last night was not such a big deal. The media loves blowing things out of proportion, especially that Ramona Vakil . . . You know this better than all of us.'

'No big deal? No big deal . . . They've called her a *Wannabe Fashionista* . . . My daughter, a wannabe . . . gawd! Do you even realize what this has done to my reputation?'

'It's always about you Kajol, isn't it?' Sulu's icy remark stuns Mom mid shriek. She locks eyes with Sulu. I glimpse a flicker of fear and then it's gone.

'Yes it is, and it better be about me, Sulu. I have slaved really, really hard to get where I am today and I am not going to let a stupid, idiot kid mess it up for me . . . no way!'

My heart stops beating.

Is that what Mom really thinks of me? An idiot, who has messed up her life! The ground begins spinning wildly. Everything's a blur; my breath is faint.

'She's just angry, that's all,' whispers an anxious voice. 'No, she's not, she HATES YOU!' snarls another. 'She wishes you were never born!' I am shaking with fear and anger, ready to explode.

'That stupid idiot happens to be *your* child, Kajol. In case you've conveniently forgotten . . .'

The barb strikes home, deep. Mom flushes. She strides across angrily to Sulu, and just when I think I am going to witness a ghastly Dexter moment, Mom loses her nerve and flings her most treasured baccarat vase at the bay window instead, narrowly missing our forever-late help, Laxmibai, who was at that very moment trying to sneak in unseen.

Laxmibai promptly brings the house down with her dreadful shrieking. Grabbing the god-sent opportunity, she accuses Mom of trying to kill her, turns tail in her navari sari and runs off leaving behind a mountain of chores.

'Hey, come back, you wretched woman. Don't you know who I am!'

'See everything is always about you, always!' Sulu is still spitting fire.

'And you're the *perfect* person to preach, aren't you now, Ms Sulochana?' snorts back Mom. 'Look at yourself, always getting into trouble for those naked, hideous paintings you insist on doing! And how dare you talk to me about being selfish when you plonked me in boarding school and jazzed off with that smelly Dieter? I was only ten years old . . . .you were never, ever there for me!'

My head is pounding and my stomach writhing in agony. I rush to my bedroom, slam it shut and dashing into the washroom, retch my guts out. Mom's contemptuous words keep ringing, 'You are a Wannabe Fashionista!'

I want to die.

* * *

'Angie, Angie! Open the door now. Don't make me break it down!' Sulu's been pounding on my door for the last half an hour now. They've finally stopped screaming at each other but Mom's contemptuous voice keeps intoning, 'Wannabe Fashionista', 'Stupid, idiot kid,' a stuck record, over and over and over in my head mocking me.

'You are a stupid, idiot kid; can't even do a simple suicide right,' a voice sneaks in. My body begins shivering, shaking as these thoughts begin to swirl around tantalizingly, each one more outrageous than the other. Terrible plans are shaping up inside my head.

'Angie, it's me Sam. Open the door right now, we need to talk!' The darkness slowly lifts, I find my breath again. It's my

BF. 'Listen babes, open the door. You're not going to believe what happened at school today. It's about Roberto . . . open the door and I'll tell you.'

Anger suddenly surges through me. How dare she make fun of my situation! I fling open the door, 'You think that by just saying *Roberto* I'm going to jump up and down with joy!'

'Well, you did get up and open the door, right?' Sam's worried eyes try and smile. She quickly enters my room and shuts Sulu out. 'Look Angie, Sulu told me what happened last night with your mom. We all know how insensitive aunty can be. But locking yourself up for hours, frightening everybody like this, over a stupid thing she said, it's not worth it.'

'Sam, I'm in the bloody news; they're calling me a *Wannabe Fashionista*! Look at what they've written about me. And Mom called me stupid, idiot kid! I want to kill myself, Sam!' I suddenly burst out crying.

Sam stares at me in shock. She's never seen this side of me. I'm her hero. I NEVER CRY. I make others cry. She quickly recovers and hugs me tight.

'Look babes, you're in the NEWS . . . . Yes it's for the wrong reasons but hey, *any* publicity is good publicity! Besides, your options of knocking yourself off are severely limited.'

Sam draws herself up to an imperious five feet no inches, sucking in her omnipresent paunch, thanks to the million rasogullas downed on the sly over the years. Long, thick hair askew, Sam looks like a mini messiah on a mission. She begins to tick off my suicide options on her chubby fingers very seriously.

'First of all, you can't hang yourself coz you don't have a ceiling fan thanks to central air conditioning, don't own a decent dupatta 'coz you hate Indian outfits, and your bedsheets are fitted so one can't knot them easily.

'Second, jumping from a balcony will only break your leg, neck or worst case your spine, so then spending your life in a wheelchair is not the grandest thing in the long run.'

I shift uneasily. Damn, I hate it how she can read my mind!

'Lastly, the very idea of guzzling down stinky rat poison or leaping off the Bandra Sea Link into our horribly polluted Arabian Sea is quite frankly a thoroughly disgusting prospect! So I honestly believe that you better rethink this whole melodrama business of knocking yourself off over a measly wardrobe malfunction . . .'

'How dare you make fun of me, Sam! You, of all people, should understand how I'm feeling!' I burst out feeling really furious.

Sam calmly hands me the tissue box.

'It's just a silly fashion blooper, that's all Angie. Come on get real.' Sam shrugs. 'Imagine the headlines; "Fashionista kills self over wrong dress." I mean seriously? Kill yourself over something worthwhile like a Lamborghini or Robert Pattinson if you must.' My eyes pop out at her audacity.

Sam's thrilled with the effect she's had on me. It's usually the other way around with me lending her my shoulder or tissues or whatever else is at hand. Last time it was my new

Zara miniskirt which she wept into. I can't believe she's got the cheek to walk into my room and mock me at a time like this; must be the effect of that preachy motivational course she attended recently. And because she's my BF, I continue to sniff and snort and snivel away. Soon enough, I begin tossing aside all thoughts of strangulations, poisons and jumping; my life suddenly seems too comical to be taken seriously even by me! I take a really deep breath, give her a big hug and feel those ominous dark thoughts fade away instantly.

'You know Sam, you're right. I'm not going to let Mom's comments bother me. Naw, I think I'll just go and get myself another tattoo.' I wink, lift my top a little and show her the freshly inked devil on my hip bone!

'You didn't! When did you? Oh My God! Has aunty seen it?' Messiah Sam's having a major cardiac arrest. I grin. I am enjoying myself again.

'Don't be silly I don't go around flashing my hips at Mom. She'll see it only when we go to Phuket this winter, and only *if* I wear a bikini . . .' We burst out laughing.

A bit about our relationship: I've been Sam's only friend at the stuffy, snooty Royal International School for the past two years. What really sparked her undying devotion to me was when I walked in on her getting mauled by Nikki and her preppie gang in the loo. I had let loose a volley of very colourful expletives, picked up Sam's books, dried her tears, rearranged her confidence and soon Sam had joined Angie Kulkarni on the far left bench way at the back of the class. Of course her parents had lectured her on why, based on the number of my detentions, suspensions, grade calculations and not to mention my filmy background; how she would be better off *without* me, that I was toxic trouble and all that parenting jazz to make sure their offspring didn't turn into a juvenile delinquent. But Sam's a pure soul, so dumping someone who had saved her from bathroom bullies wasn't even an option. Besides, she is as crazy about fashion as I am. Well, not as nuts as me, but bonkers enough to raid Fashion Street with me every Saturday.

She picks up my sketchbook that's lying on my table and flips it open. 'Angie, these new designs are amazing!' she gasps, staring at the drawings. 'Gosh, now this does make you wanna kill someone . . .' She laughs, picking up the ensemble that's got me into trouble.

'So true,' I laugh along when a crazy thought strikes me. I can't kill myself, but I sure can annihilate the object of my misery, right? And then as if in a dream, I pick up my scissors, grab the dress out of Sam's hands.

'This is for all the fashionistas in the world, don't let anyone steal your style!' a voice whispers in my head and a slashing sound rents the air . . .

Sam screams and tries to stop me, 'What are you *doing?* You've gone mad, Angie!' I would have made Johnny Depp proud as Angie Scissor Hands. Within half an hour, the fluffy frufru dress was shredded to itsy-bitsy bits . . . The moment where I was in charge of my anger snipping away was *totally* glorious. Quite predictably my euphoria lasted precisely till the next morning.

3

BFF (BEST FRIENDS FOREVER)

There are usually two types of grandmothers—the snowy-haired, sugary-sweet ones that turn up for every family do laden with completely useless gifts, constantly squish you on to their saggy bosom, pull your cheeks and then, proceed to blackmail you into serving them for a lifetime.

'Bachha, zara please get me a samosa, a cup of garam chai etc. . . .' Venky's Kanjeevaram-encased grandma is a direct descendent of this sneaky breed.

The second kind is the cold, unrelenting, hug-me-not variety who eye you with utter disdain, barely acknowledge your existence, purposely announcing your miserable grades to the entire world just to make you feel like a worthless insect and then *still* manage to bully you into serving them samosa and chai *and* washing their dentures!

Poor Sam is saddled with this specimen of a dragon.

So when Sulu turned up on our doorstep last year all

silver haired and gypsy styled, grandly gatecrashing Mom's birthday party to reconnect with her only child after decades of globetrotting, I was at first terrified and then completely overwhelmed. Sulochona Saxena just didn't fit the grandma profile. A week into our lives and she hadn't pinched my cheeks, hadn't dissected my grades, hadn't given me the usual spiel on how much prettier I'd look if I'd lose some weight, had loved my kooky fashion sketches and most amazing act of all—had stayed out of my closet!

Sulu is a grandma made in heaven. She's my guardian angel. And yet today, I avoid her and quickly dash off to school without giving her our ritual bear hug. Hurt, she smiles wistfully and waves me off.

* * *

'All okay at home?' Sam pounces on me near the lockers during lunch break. 'Anything happened last night? I hope you didn't do something stupid.' Closet secret—Sam's a psychotic angel and needling someone repeatedly is definitely one of her crazy traits (Okay . . . she's not really psycho but she does go overboard pretty often).

'No, I didn't do anything *stupid* okay!' My voice rises sharply, startling Venky, who has been hanging around holding on to Sam's sleeve, trying to catch my attention.

'Hi Angie, am sorry I didn't hear your calls, was really busy practising for my concert. Mozart's Piano Concerto No. 15 in B-flat major and Beethoven's Piano Sonata No. 29 are just crazy tough!' he begins rattling off nervously, his face all sweaty and anxious. Sometimes I feel Royal International School should have insisted on uniforms for its students; this would have spared us the horrendously hideous, geeky permutations and combinations Venky always comes up with. And as much as I have tried to help him on this issue, Venky invariably has a fatal fashion relapse every single morning.

'Yeah, well as you have no time for me I'm afraid I won't be going to your frigging, stuffy piano concert,' I hiss nastily.

He drops his books in utter shock, splattering them all over the floor; people are stopping and glancing our way. I completely ignore him. How dare he put pesky piano practice before me! Doesn't he get the importance of *twelve* missed calls? I mean come on . . .!

'Hey! We're just concerned, okay? That's all, so quit making a blooming scene, Angie,' Sam pulls me aside. 'Get a grip on yourself, babes!'

A burst of mocking laughter startles us out of our little spat. It's none other than Nikita Vakil, Ramona's nasty daughter, the school diva, and her gang. This looks like trouble, big trouble.

'So wassup, huh? Looks to me like these BFs are having a little catfight, huh?'

Nikki is smirking, her gang giggling like a pack of wolves. And quite insanely all I can think of at this moment is how I wish I looked like her. Fair, confident, slim, pouty, sexy, foxy . . .

'So our very own Angie is in the news these days . . . umm, what do we now call you? Ah yes, a *Wannabe Fashionista!*'

Nikki has a sharp, high-pitched voice that carries far and wide especially when she's bitching about someone. Sure enough, a crowd starts gathering for the show. The twitter of snickers snowballs into a loud explosion of laughter.

I straighten up and lock eyes with my arch enemy, hoping my cold, hard, kohl stare will wilt her into shutting up, when I suddenly spy out of the corner of my eye—the utterly luscious Roberto Missoni heading our way!

* * *

It's been less than a month since the Italian diplomat's son joined Royal International, and every girl from kindergarten to high school now suffers from accelerated heartbeats every time he appears on the horizon. Including, yours truly.

Predictably the ruthless Nikki Vakil zeroed in on him like a ravenous tarantula, her superior social climbing skills courtesy a high-profile lawyer father and Bollywood talk-show anchor mother. By the weekend, Nikki had dumped her current beau Karan Oberoi and his Porsche like a pack of soggy potato chips and nabbed an exclusive coffee date with Roberto. On Monday, Madame Tarantula had updated her FB status from 'Love Punjabi Parathas' to 'Adore Pepperoni Pizza'.

Nikki never let her Italian obsession out of her sight. She followed him everywhere from cafeteria cooler to car park, tottering dangerously on her Jimmy Choos. But that didn't stop the hopefuls from trying to lure him away with all sorts of feminine wiles. All hearts fell—except Sam, the one girl who disliked Roberto with a vengeance. Her reason, the

Italian was too good looking to be trustworthy! And this logic to me bordered on the really, utterly ridiculous.

'He's such a *faku*; just mark my words, Angie,' Sam remarked. 'I overhead him giving a tear-jerker of an excuse for missing five submissions last week. And he actually got starchy Subramaniam Ma'am all weepy! Don't be fooled by those chocolate boy looks. These kinda guys just love themselves and absolutely no one else,' Sam added grimly.

But in spite of Sam's dire warnings all I remember are the two whole minutes when Roberto had stopped by my canvas during art class, looked into my eyes and said my work reminded him of Warhol. Flattered and thrilled, I too was struck by the charming Italian virus. So now if I have to stay on his radar, I must stop Roberto from heading our way. I've gotta stop Nikki from yakking on and on about me.

But Nikki is relentless, and she goes for my jugular, her voice rising higher and higher.

'I pity you. You must have such a tough time with an actress as a mother,' she mocks. 'Always away on shoots, no time for poor little Angie. Just *look* at you . . . your hair, your weight, your clothes . . . why, you don't even look like her!' Nikita shakes her head sadly, mournfully. 'I mean honestly guys, what *is* this?' And then my stomach turns. She's got my secret design sketchbook! Oh god! I must have forgotten to put it away in my locker after maths class! The wretched girl is waving it around. Now everyone's crowding around, looking at MY SECRETS! Some of them pointing and giggling!

'This, everyone, is called Bag lady fashion,' Nikki points disparagingly to my fishnet stockings, fur-trimmed boots and oversized neon jumper. 'Stuff that only wannabe fashionistas wear. Me dahlings, I wouldn't be caught dead in this kind of trash . . .'

That does it. I lose it. Roberto or no Roberto, no one talks to me like this!

'Listen Miss Gucci Pucci, at least I have the guts to wear originals instead of Bangkok fakes! Don't get me started on your hazaar diets—and we all know about your protein milkshakes. One more word about my Mom and I'll . . .'

'We'll both knock your teeth out!' Sam is right beside me, shaking like a leaf, but her voice is clear and strong. She's holding my right hand tightly, fists clenched, ready to swing into action. Dear god, I'm so close to losing my cool and throwing some really nasty MMA punches at Nikita when Venky reaches out for my left hand forcing me to calm down.

Roberto's joined the circus, his handsome face guarded as he tries to figure out why on earth is Nikki neck deep in a catfight.

'And you'll do what, Ms Geetanjali Kulkarni? Huh? You're a loser and so are your weirdo friends. All the best with your ridiculous designs . . . Know what? Your kinds will always be Wannabe Fashionistas!' spits out Nikki. Then, she makes that one fatal mistake; she tosses my sketchbook contemptuously into the air. I watch the pages tear away and my precious designs scatter on to the floor. Red hot anger grips my innards and as she begins to turn away, I can no longer feel my right arm. A sharp sound stings the air as shocked silence follows.

I have slapped Nikita Vakil, sending her flying to the floor.

* * *

It was a wonder our principal, Nalini Ma'am, didn't expel us, especially when there was an entire mob vouching that I had gone completely bananas. Add liberal doses of drama-queen theatrics, a bunch of false allegations, and the bully is now the poor victim.

'It's only a week's suspension Angie, that's all,' assures Sam. 'In any case, my parents don't really care. By the time they return from Europe, this will blow over. Dad will hold back a week's allowance, Mom will pretend to be angry and by dawn, they'd have forgotten and started to pack their bags for another trip.' She shrugs nonchalantly, trying hard to hide the hurt that comes with being the least priority item with parents who are too busy building empires. 'Angie, It's *you* I'm worried about.'

Sam's right. How on earth am I going to now explain this new development to Mom? She'll murder me for sure! Maybe I'll just come down with a fever or something. But faking a fever for one whole week was going to be pretty tough.

How about a mysterious headache? How long does a migraine last, huh?

Or a stomach ache? Can't blame the school cafeteria, it's way too hygienic!

I wrack my brains desperately. What am I going to tell her?

'Should I try and get myself suspended as well?' Venky squeaks. 'Maybe flunk the physics test?'

Venky is severely depressed. Thanks to his genius standing, he was let off with a mere warning and now he's going to be all alone at school without us to watch his back. Plus, we all know that a lot can happen in a single week at school when you're minus your friends. It's a scary prospect.

'How about me flunking maths, physics and chemistry . . .?'

We burst out laughing, startling the watchman who is busy rounding up student stragglers. 'Abhi ghar jao,' he warns us. 'Jaldi karo,' he frowns, blowing his whistle impatiently. 'School band hai.'

'Venky, even if you tried really, really hard, maybe even go for it blindfolded, you just can't flunk!' I pick up my bag and begin walking to the gate. 'You're just too smart for your own good buddy.'

'I guess I'll just pretend I'm off to school and land up at Sam's place and hang around till it's time to go home . . .' he mumbles following me. Sam and I stop and stare at each other in amazement.

'That's totally brilliant, Venky!' My heart is singing with joy. 'That way no one at home will find out. That's what I'm going to do!'

'Hey! You can't do that Angie, that's lying! You've gotta tell . . .' he protests weakly. 'Oh god, what have I done?'

I impulsively hug Venky, squashing the breath out of him, shutting him up from making me change my mind . . . It's a brilliant plan and he doesn't know that he's just saved my . . . ☺

4

OFTB (OUT OF THE BLUE)

Mercifully Mom was out of town for a week on a shoot. Dad was busy at work, and in any case apart from waking me up in the morning to make sure I did the mandatory twelve surya namaskars, pranayam and the half-hour bike ride to burn 300 calories off my podgy body, he would come home really late in the evening all tired out from the new merger he's working on. As for Sulu, she didn't suspect a thing. My awesome grandma was so upset after THE BIG FIGHT with Mom that she gifted me Cheetos, a diva of a tabby, saying, 'Angie one must always be like a cat: cool and composed no matter how loud the dogs bark.'

Cheetos is truly Ms Attitude. The cat's got style, nose up in the air if she doesn't like anything, a disdainful whisk of her tail if you pass a nasty remark about her increasing voluptuousness, and finally the swift, sharp claws if you dare cross the limit with her. Yup I now have a cat for a guru!

But in time, even the best-laid plans can go wrong say the Ancients, and sure enough three days into our devilish plans, I get stumped by the most unexpected visitor who turns up on my doorstep after school. Chotu, our man Friday, was snoozing post lunch, Laxmibai was playing truant as usual, and I was listening to music, leafing through the latest *Vogue* when the doorbell rang and turned my world upside down.

'Ciao Roberto, what a surprise! Come in.'

Nope I'm not fibbing! And yes I'm secretly learning Italian online, and Ciao is actually both hello and goodbye (bet you didn't know that, huh?)

Can he hear my heart pounding really hard? I take a few quick breaths, trying to look cool and composed. Act normal, I tell myself, like great-looking dudes drop by your home all the time. Are all Italians this gorgeous, whispers my mind.

'Ciao Angie, what's up? Hope I'm not disturbing you.' His European accent burring into an American drawl almost gives me goosebumps. Roberto makes himself comfortable on the sofa flashing the perfect smile that knocks my knees out, sends my adrenaline pumping and makes my palms sweat. Cool-and-composed Angie goes flying out of the window in a jiffy.

'So how does it feel being in the news these days, being followed by the paparazzi?'

'Well, umm,' I begin to sputter, trying to conjure up the perfect witty answer. Don't you dare screw this up! 'It's not a big thingee, really, just kinda happened . . .' I shrug nonchalantly trying to look really chilled out. Why is he here? Has he lost his way? That's ridiculous. He's just two streets down the road. Maybe he's just taking a walk. Roberto's next words send my world exploding.

'I think your designs are pretty cool. It takes guts to be different, to do what no one else is doing, you know what I mean? Too bad you got into trouble.'

Am I hearing right? I pinch myself. Yup, I'm not dreaming. Should I record this for posterity? Uno momento . . . is he here to blackmail me? After all he *is* Italian. Is he from the mafia? The thought makes my blood run cold.

'Look Roberto, my parents don't know about me being suspended . . .' I whisper hoarsely, hoping Sulu isn't in the next room. 'So please don't tell.'

'No way, I'm not here to get you into trouble. I'm just amazed that you are such a great artiste. (I love the way he says that word!) 'Me . . . I love art but just can't seem to draw or paint anything nice,' he smiles.

Just then Cheetos saunters over, makes her way to Roberto and takes a fancy to his shoes! Before I know it, he's picked Cheetos up gently and she's actually purring in his arms!

'She's beautiful, is she Persian? My Mom loves cats; we're going to adopt a couple here as well.'

'I think Cheetos is a stray. My grandmother gifted her to me few days ago, and she's already put on too much weight.' Isn't it amazing that he loves cats? I think to myself.

'Who says you're fat, Cheetos? Tell them these curves are to die for,' he grins and playfully lifts Cheetos high, overhead. His tee rides up and I catch a glimpse of washboard abs, those lovely lean muscles, tanned skin and my mouth goes dry. He catches my gaze. I blush furiously looking away. What does Roberto want? Why is he here?

Mercifully Chotu comes in squinting disapprovingly, carrying a tray of his delectable frothy cold coffees, piping hot samosas and green mint chutney.

'I not feeling well,' he snaps churlishly banging the tray down to indicate his disapproval of our guest. Cheetos is suitably spooked and flees to my room. I spend ten minutes reassuring our nosey man Friday in Hindi that the phirangi is just a classmate delivering school notes and that he has no intentions of outraging my modesty. And of course Chotu needn't stand guard outside the door just in case . . .

I watch Roberto covertly. Dear god, even the way he eats is divine . . . I'm lost in his blue eyes when his next words jolt me out of my stupor. He's handing me something.

'I think this is yours? Si Cara?' he hands me my sketchbook, tattered but still intact! I almost burst into tears; I thought I had lost it for good during the fight.

'Angie.' His voice is soooo hypnotic, I am rapt.

'I hope you don't mind but I took a look at your designs. They are very interesting—the colour palette, the cuts, very unusual, very different; just like you. I really like the flair and funkiness in your designs. They are really neat! You are definitely a fashionista.'

I nod dumbstruck. Am I hearing right? The very stylish Italian Roberto Missoni has just anointed me, Angie Kulkarni, a fashionista!

My head is swimming; I'm drowning in his blue eyes, falling helplessly into the depths of infatuation . . .

'Have you heard of Teen Runway Contest by the House of Verduce?' Roberto is speaking. I snap back to the present hastily.

Who in the world of fashion hasn't? The Teen Runaway Contest by the House of Verduce was launched last year in memory of Mario Verduce the twenty-five-year-old maverick designer and heir who had just committed suicide. The suicide note revealed that Mario had taken this tragic step after a malicious fashion critic had questioned Verduce's talent following three consecutive disastrous runway shows. I still remember that awful day, I had been so shattered.

'Yes, of course I have. I totally love Mario Verduce's designs! They are so inspiring! I've collected each and every one of his sketches,' I blurt out impulsively.

'Yes, he was fantastic, wasn't he?' Sadness clouds Roberto's face. 'Mario was my cousin and my godfather.'

I sit shocked, frozen as Roberto grapples with the pain of memories. And then he's back, emotions steeled and controlled.

'Well, this year, the Italian Embassy and the House of Verduce are co-hosting the Teen Runway Contest, and it is open to contestants from various countries including India. Participants have six weeks to prepare three designs sketches for the preliminary round: Evening wear, Formal and Casual. The top six designers selected will fly to Italy for a week and stay at the House of Verduce where they must create their

'Teen Runway Showstopper.' The grand prize is the chance to intern for an entire year at the House of Verduce. All expenses paid! When my Mom mentioned it yesterday, I immediately thought of you. You're pretty good, maybe you should give Teen Runway a shot.'

At this point my jaw slams into the floor. Is this for real? Roberto Missoni thought of me . . . That I should take part! Of course yes, YES! I almost scream. But then I shrug coolly and say, 'Okay, sounds like a plan,' instead. This is insane! My mind is already racing with a zillion designs. This is my dream come true, my chance to shine and to show Mom that I do have a sense of fashion.

Roberto looks at me a bit puzzled. Okay, I should have reacted a bit warmer than a snowflake but there was the serious danger of me screaming hysterically and flinging myself at his feet, a not so cool thingee . . . Right?

'Your designs are very good. I think you can win this, Angie.' You think! What else do you think about me Roberto?

'This is my number; call me and let me know quickly so I can get the entry form for you.' I quickly save his number in my cell phone.

'Ciao Cara.' He shakes my hand, our fingers brush briefly. I have died and gone to heaven.

* * *

Normally one would charge off to tell the BFs about an earth-shattering, life-changing event like this one, right? Well, I don't. Dunno why. I sit in the spot Roberto has warmed up, breathing in his scent, memorizing his cell number till I know it backwards. 'Your designs are very good. You can win this.' His voice sings all night long to me as I sketch away furiously, bitten badly by the love bug.

Well, I will tell Sam and Venky, just not yet. So I hug this little secret, wait for suspension to get over, and four days later, saunter back to school as if nothing's happened. But a lot has indeed changed. For me.

Dad is pleasantly surprised that he doesn't have to poke and prod me into waking up early in the morning any more and that I've suddenly developed an aversion to vada pav and an obsession with broccoli. Mom's kinda thawed a bit after she found me studying two nights in a row instead of poring through fashion magazines. The only person really disturbed by the *new* me is Sulu.

'What's going on, Angie?' She accosts me as I come home that afternoon. 'Why aren't you hanging out with Sam and Venky any more? What's all this with the dieting and exercising? Something happened? You wanna talk?'

'Nothing's happened, Sulu. Just that I really, really need to lose this weight.'

I lie. I'm not ready to share secrets right now, not with Sulu or anyone.

'You know Angie, you're a lousy liar. It's that diplomat's son. Roberto, isn't that his name? I know the kind. Good looks, they use their charm, flatter you, say you're special, steal your heart and make you lose your mind. Be careful.'

Her eyes bore into me. Sulu's remarks have hit a raw nerve; I am tired and my temper flares.

'Roberto's not like that, okay? Roberto really, really likes me, and what's more he likes my designs!' My voice rises, high-pitched, tensed; for deep down Nikki is still his arm candy, and I'm only a hopeful candidate. I grow reckless. And throwing sense to the winds, I blurt out shocking myself . . . 'Roberto has just asked me to the school prom . . . beat that!'

And with that Angie Kulkarni is now officially in deep doo-doo.

5

XOXO (KNOTS & CROSSES— WHAT DID YOU THINK?)

With new friends entering your life, old pals and their predictabilities begin to annoy you no end.

You no longer find their Santa Banta jokes funny; you ease off liking their FB updates, you no longer text them every detail of your day, you stop planning to hang out in the evenings after school and pretty soon, you're begging off lunch break with bizarre excuses like wanting to study, that you're on a no-carb diet or need to meditate . . . In short, you make yourself scarce. And then eventually, cross them out.

First puzzled, then pissed off, Sam and Venky accost me two days later just as I've sat down to lunch with Roberto. The school prom, the most happening event in the school calendar, is just two weeks away and after eight WhatsApp messages, I've bagged today's solo lunch date on the pretext of getting his opinions on some sketches of the prom dress

I'm designing. I'm hoping he'll get the hint. Oh, never mind if it's in the school cafeteria with everyone eavesdropping; I'm running out of time and have gotta nail it today before Madame Tarantula beats me to it!

'Angie, we need to talk . . .' It's a very determined Sam locking eyes with me. 'In *private* . . .' She gestures to an empty table across the room. Venky stands beside her glaring through his specs, trying very hard to get an evil glint in his eyes. But he looks all bug eyed and weird instead! By now an ominous silence has engulfed the cafeteria; everyone's waiting for the mother of all battles—the BF Showdown. Yup, us three not hanging out any more, is the latest gossip buzzing on the grapevine. I am in the news once more.

'I'm busy, as you can see; we're discussing our art assignment right now. I'll catch you after school, okay?' I say imperiously, putting my sandwich down very deliberately and glare at Sam. How dare they barge in like this? Has Sam lost her brains? The clock's ticking away; the following class is maths with Madame Tarantula sitting next to Roberto for two whole periods! Next art class is three days away; I've got just twenty minutes to grab Roberto's attention before I lose my nerve to pop the question.

Puzzled, Roberto looks first at me, then at the irate Sam. He quickly stands up, pushing his plate away and picking up his books—chance ruined!

'No, no we're not discussing anything important at all. Why don't you guys sort things out . . . hmmm? Angie, I've got library period now. Catch you later. Bye, *a dopo*!' Roberto flashes his devastating smile and makes a hasty exit.

CATCH ME LATER!!! *WHEN*?

The wretched prom's two weeks away, I've got broccoli coming out of my ears, my weight hasn't budged a gram and I've possibly lost my only chance to ask him out . . . I'm so furious, I can't even breathe. I turn on Sam, my temper rising with every minute.

'Drat it, Sam! What do you want? Just stop following me around, okay? I've had enough of you guys . . . just leave me the hell ALONE!'

Sam stands there shocked—crumbling, trembling, shattered and devastated. Her eyes say it all. But her voice is icy with hate.

'Sure Angie. That's what we'll do from now on, leave you the hell alone!'

* * *

Being ALONE is really scary.

Let no adult fool you into believing that 'spending time with yourself reflecting on issues' helps you mature as a person. It's all BS; we humans need a comforting shoulder or two to lean on in difficult times. A good solid one you can bawl your lungs out on, and I am currently in a really dreadful shoulder-less pickle.

Sulu is away for a fortnight at some artist retreat. Mom's too busy gearing up for the Oscars to lend me her shoulder. Dad's shoulder is usually at work or overseas. The gang's shoulders are now completely out of the question. And it's rather difficult to bawl on one's own shoulder.

How am I going to get Roberto to ask me out?

Call him.

What if he thinks you're desperate?

But you are desperate, aren't you? Sam's voice whispers like always, reassuring, but fades away just as I begin to listen.

Oh god! Why did I have to go and muck things up with Sam and Venky? Sam always has the perfect solutions to all my problems, however outlandish her advice usually is. And as for Venky—he's like a Labrador: ever faithful and devoted in spite of my sometimes nasty and often erratic behaviour towards him. Suddenly I feel small, really guilty. I miss them soooo very much, their quirkiness and unconditional friendship. My heart aches as Adele croons *Sky Fall,* our fave song, bringing back all the fun times we've shared.

But when, Roberto and I had our first official coffee date (okay . . . it was more like him handing me the contest form and me insisting on treating him to coffee) at the Starbucks near my home where we ended up chatting for two hours. I remember how gloriously the first hour was chugging along. We laughed, discussed and debated our favourite designers as well as fashion trends, and then I asked what he thought about the Indian fashion scene.

'Well Cara, no offence but fashion here is so over the top. Sometimes it's too much! Colour, glitter, sequins everywhere! There's so much of mixing of prints happening, it's crazy! No offence but take your friend Venky, for example. Yesterday he turned up in a striped shirt with checked pants! What next!' Roberto laughed.

I squirmed in silence, embarrassed once again by Venky's wretched wardrobe disasters.

'Now I quite like Sam's spunky clothes; they go well with her do-or-die attitude. Though she can tone it down a bit . . . Now you, Angie, you know how to work colours and prints cleverly; they should learn a thing or two from you.' He wasn't being mean or anything, just voicing his opinion.

My coffee lost its flavour and I promptly decided to drop my BFs there and then . . . Truth is—I was so desperate to be with Roberto, soaking in his incredible handsomeness that I said nothing in their defence, never once told him about Sam's amazing voice that sounds just like Adele and how Venky's fashion-challenged fingers can make *your* Ferragamos dance to his piano tunes. Never even mentioned how deep our friendship is, that it goes way beyond the superficial hanging out together.

Suddenly I'm ashamed at what I've done to us. Thank god realization has dawned soon! I pick up my cell and dial Sam's number. My heart's pounding and yes, I'm beyond terrified. What if they don't want me back? Would serve me right . . .

'Hey Sam . . . could you come over? I need to talk to you . . . Look, I'm really, really sorry about . . .' Click! The phone goes dead.

* * *

Fortunately three hours later with Sam raging on like a bull in a China shop over my atrocious un-buddy like behaviour, we are pretty much back to normal. Venky is so relieved he begins humming a Mozart sonata which Sam and I promptly drown out by pumping up *Titanium* by Sia. When suddenly I remember the mess I am in, and all the happiness fizzles out of me. I flop down on the floor with a thud.

'Roberto shouldn't be the end of your world, Angie,' says Sam gently holding out a luscious slice of pepperoni pizza. I bite into it eagerly; it's been one long, miserable, dreadful no-pizza week, and I'm about to die of fat denial. 'Anyway, he's just not your cup of tea . . . he's so full of himself . . .' she starts revving up to begin bashing Roberto all over again. Suddenly the pizza loses its taste.

'No, he's not! He's really, really nice okay?' I protest. I've had enough of everyone running Roberto down. 'You guys don't know him like *I* do.'

'Oh pray, do tell us what Roberto Missoni's *really* like, we're all ears!' Sam takes a long sip of her Coke and challenges me.

* * *

Venky sits dazed while Sam struggles to control her disbelief as I narrate in detail the totally curious incident of Roberto coming home to return my sketchbook, telling me that he loves my designs, and then insisting that I take part in the Teen Runway design contest! At this point Sam goes into total shock.

'The famous Teen Runway Contest? Hosted by the Verduce Fashion House?' she squawks disbelievingly.

'Yup, that's the one, and Roberto thinks I could actually win the contest!'

Just recollecting it all has given me goosebumps.

Silence follows my bombshell of a confession. Sam quickly recovers and begins pacing the floor while Venky is still in shock. He begins polishing his specs furiously.

'All right then, BF. I'll give this Missoni character a chance. But here's what we need to figure out. There is no doubt that our Angie will create the perfect dress, we have the perfect occasion for that perfect dress but strangely, the perfectly charming Missoni after all the attention and hints is yet to ask her to the ball!' Sam swivels around abruptly. A sudden thought has struck her. 'Oh my god! Is he gay?'

'His name's Roberto not Missoni. And no, he's not gay!' I hiss through clenched teeth. She's riling me up for another spat. Venky shakes his head, warning me to keep my cool. 'He's with Nikki, remember? And they've kissed. He told me.' I fib, hoping to shut her up.

'WHAAAT! The cad's telling you that he has been necking with her. That's just not done!'

'Sam . . . please calm down . . .' Venky quickly butts in, hoping to ward off another ugly spat.

'Yeah, you're right, Venks. Take a deep breath, Sam. Relax. And think!' she mutters to herself, plonking herself on to my bed, closes her eyes and launches into a noisy pranayama that scares a couple of lives out of Cheetos. Our

Sam swings from one mood to another like a trapeze artist. 'This is a tough one. Missoni's not gay, but just plain dumb not to take an obvious hint. So now we've got to somehow get Missoni alone so that Angie can ask him out.'

'Dunno about asking him out.' All my earlier cafeteria bravado has suddenly evaporated and I'm not quite sure about this whole *asking him* out business. 'Maybe Venky can slip him a note or something . . .' I look at Venky pleading.

'A Note? *A Note!* Are you crazy? There is no time for a note, girl! It's a do-or-die scenario!' Sam is back on that trapeze again. This is getting totally out of hand! Forget about going to the blooming prom as his date. I'll just lurk around the dance floor hoping Roberto will ask me for a dance out of pity. Suddenly Sam turns and grabs me, a wild excited look in her eyes.

'I've got it . . . This . . . is . . . what we are going to do . . .'

6

POA (PLAN OF ACTION)

Mission Missoni was not impossible . . . just highly ridiculous! But it's difficult to argue with a pint-sized, bull-headed BF when she's made up her mind to embark on the insane.

Lucky for us, Mom's busy getting ready to leave for Los Angeles, Dad's at work and Sulu's got two art exhibitions to inaugurate on the same day. We have the Kulkarni house all to ourselves.

'Don't worry Sulu. It's ok if Chotu isn't around, we're going to be revising algebra and trigonometry, right Venky? And these guys will hang around till you return,' I quickly assure my grandma; she hates it if I'm home alone for too long.

I hug her really tight while Sam and Venky give her these extra cheery byes. I can tell that she knows that we're up to some mischief, but she can't do much about it as she's the chief guest at both events. Sulu's car turns the corner and joins the frenzied Mumbai traffic and within seconds of her face vanishing from sight, Sam takes charge.

'All right, listen up you two. Venky, quit shaking! Everyone has to give in their couple names by day after, right? And every couple must go in person to register with Ms Subramaniam, right? So we have just one *single* window of opportunity to strike— sports practice tomorrow after school.' My stomach instantly begins churning as Sam unfolds her devious plan.

'Every evening after school, Tarantula is perched on the soccer ringside bleachers sipping green tea from her flask, keeping a beady eye on Missoni during his one-hour soccer practice. She always leaves her seat ten minutes prior to practice ending and heads for the washroom to doll up before they go off to CCD to koochie coo.'

I'm truly impressed. Sam has done her homework well. I listen in more intently.

'Venky . . . here's where you come in.'

Before Venky can even squawk out a protest, Sam snares him by the neck.

'You will find a seat next to Tarantula and chat her up. Pretend you're smitten by her, offer to do her homework, ask her about her favourite film, anything and then . . . when she's not looking, open her flask and drop this in her drink.' Sam pulls out a tiny packet. Venky jumps up alarmed. 'Don't worry, it's only a laxative powder. Stole it from my granny; nothing serious but enough to get Tarantula's tummy turning.'

'This is insane; I'm not doing this . . . ouch!' Venky squawks out a protest. 'Do it yourself.'

'Listen butthead, you're the only one from our gang she doesn't notice at all.'

'Hey! That's not fair; Nikki smiled at me yesterday during chemistry. She admires my genius . . . .'

A not-so-gentle tweak by Sam on the Venky earlobe and it's, 'Okay, okay, I will do it, just this once!'

'Good, now listen up. The minute her tummy turns, offer to walk her to the ladies room, wait for her to enter the loo and then lock her in!' Sam slams her fist into her palm, making us jump.

Have I created a monster?

'As soon as you give me a thumbs up signal, Angie will saunter over to Missoni and tell him she desperately needs a ride home as she's feeling faint. Once you're in the car with your dude, Angie, you will ruthlessly bat your eyelashes and ask him out to the prom.'

Sam's insane! 'Bat my eyelashes, what next? Pout away like a moron . . . I'm out of here!' But wild-eyed Sam grabs me by the arm.

'Trust me babes . . . this is your only chance to get rid of Tarantula. And here's the beauty of this plan . . . Even if Missoni refuses, which he will . . .'

I glare angrily at Sam. That is totally uncalled for.

'He'll have no choice but to ask you out because . . . Ta da! Thanks to Venky Madame Tarantula won't be able to make it to school the next day in time to register with him . . . . And according to school rules, everyone, and I mean, everyone must attend the school prom . . .' she lets the words sink in.

Sam's a genius!

* * *

Next day dawn, Sam pings me on WhatsApp. 'Mission Missoni here we come . . . . let's kill them!'

Sure, and I'm torn choosing between the latest lime-green pants or the electric-blue capris. Both are making my behind look larger than an elephant's. Killing everyone is going to be rather easy at this rate! I'm beginning to panic; the clock's ticking and I can't be late for art class, again. Ms Lawrence will not be amused.

I have an entire day to make sure Roberto notices me, so it's the lime-green pants paired with a black off-shoulder top to take the focus off my bottom (a fashion tip I always follow); I sling my on my favourite skull necklace when Mom pops in all yogaed out, fresh faced and cheery.

She's just back last night from a hectic two-week shoot in Switzerland for her next movie based on Mata Hari, the incredible lady spy. And yet she doesn't mind contorting herself into impossible asanas, jet-lagged but bloody determined to keep her butt from sagging. Add to that, Dad's back from Hong Kong and he's already on Marine Drive clocking his five-mile run . . . my superfit parents seriously tire me out. Why can't they just sleep in for a change? Let the fat rest a bit once in a while. Take a break from sweating away. Is cellulite sooooo important to one's happiness?

'Whoa! Someone's looking very . . .' and Mom's compliment sputters to a sudden halt.

Oh no! She's spotted the skull necklace, before I can stuff it down my bra, and her expression's rapidly morphing. She's going to say something nasty again; my heart sinks like a capsizing ship.

'Angie, why do you always have to wear those dreadful, horrid things?' her voice is rising.

'Mom, everyone's wearing them, it's just kinda cool . . . and very in right now,' I keep my voice very calm as I gather my books, avoiding her eyes, planning to escape. 'I'll be home late today. Venky's helping me with maths, okay?' I head out of my bedroom when her next remark stops me dead in my tracks.

'Hey pilloo (I love it when she uses this Marathi term for little one), Sulu told me about the Italian diplomat's son— your hot date to the school prom . . . how on earth did you manage that? Huh? I met his parents at the Indo-Italian Film Festival last week; charming couple and very elegant. Do you know that his aunt is Sophia Verduce, the famous haute couture designer? So tell me pilloo what does Roberto have to say about your crazy fashion sense, huh?' Mom's always like this, gently mocking me.

Drat it Sulu, how dare you go and tell Mom about Roberto! I wanted to surprise her after it became a reality, not now!

'Now Angie, do remember, Italians are super fashion conscious. The right label, cuts, fabrics. You should carry my

Chanel bag and let's get you a lovely dress from Suzanne; I'll call her up right now and we can meet her later when I go to check in on the clothes I'm wearing to the Oscars. And pilloo, give your magazines a rest for a while and get started on the South Beach Diet, biking and 100 surya namaskars right away to speed things up on the weight loss front, okay?'

'I'm not doing, wearing or carrying anything of yours, okay Mom,' I say silently to myself. I'm sick to the gills eating steamed swill, tired of counting every calorie burnt and now even not reading my favourite fashion magazines! That ain't happening! I love devouring every word, poring over every picture in those glam glossies! But what hurts big time, most often all the time, is Mom's automatic assumption that I'm just not Barbie enough to hook a hunk of a date! I have Tarantula and her vicious gang at school breathing down my neck, making life miserable, and there's Mom dearest at home to remind me of what a lazy bum I am. Tears well up and threaten to choke me, so before I have a complete meltdown and say things I'll regret, I simply continue walking out of the front door and slam it shut . . .

* * *

By the time school is done, I am a bundle of nerves.

'All right, Venky's in position; give him ten minutes to gather his wits, distract Tarantula, grab flask, open, make the drop and then another ten for the laxative to kick in . . .'

We've come armed with binoculars and are skulking furtively behind the banyan tree that towers at the edge of the soccer field. Mercifully almost everyone's gone home; all except the senior school soccer team. I watch Roberto weave his magic as centre forward, skilfully feinting, dodging his opponents, taking charge of the game. I sigh softly; he is Adonis incarnate.

'Get lovesick when you get him to agree to take you to the prom, not now, Miss Juliet!'

Sam swiftly trains her binoculars on the bleachers, zooming in on her prey. She's warned Venky that she'll be watching his every single move and that he had better not goof up. Poor guy's so nervous he's been running to the loo all day long. I really doubt he's going to be able to nix Tarantula. This is worse than watching *Hunger Games*!

The pressure's really getting to me. I am stinking up a storm, have run out of deo, so ready to turn tail and run home but then I glance at Sam and can't help but be a bit envious. That girl is an absolute ice bucket, not a flicker of fear, no trembling hands, nothing but a steely focus; my pint-sized BF is like a seasoned navy seal leading an attack on the Taliban! I quit sighing, tear my eyes away from the lovely vision of sweaty-muscled Roberto in his shorts and force my head back in the game.

'Come on Venky, stop stammering and get on with it!' hisses Sam impatient to lock-up our nemesis. What's going on? I hurriedly zoom in. Nikita's staring angrily at Venky, who has gone beetroot red, his eyes bulging with fear, his lips working frantically, mouthing something and his arms flapping around making him look like a clown.

'What the s . . . t is wrong with that idiot!' Sam explodes, uttering colourful curses that would have gotten us in a dump load of trouble. 'That's good . . . Distract her . . . now get out the powder . . . slowly . . . open it . . . don't spill it . . .' I've stopped breathing. I watch Nikita turn away. 'Easy does it . . .' my heart's hammering wildly, my eyes shut in fear, 'nowwww drop it . . .' Sam grabs my arm excitedly, 'Bloody hell! Our twitheads's done it!' I almost pass out in relief.

I can't believe it, we high-five each other. Then all hell breaks loose . . .

7

FATM (FOAMING AT THE MOUTH)

Karan Oberoi had decided at that very precise moment to try his luck once again with ex-girlfriend Nikita Vakil. And so, armed with a dozen roses, a new pair of stonewashed Old Navy jeans, fancy hair gel and fancier aftershave, Karan gets out of his Porsche, saunters up to the bleachers all ready to launch into a declaration of undying love and everything Valentine, when he catches Venky in the act of sneakily pouring a suspicious powder into the love of his life's drink!

Naturally, the ex-Romeo sees red and every other shade in the anger rainbow, but before Karan can reduce him to a pulpy mess, our pal Venky quickly bleats out the entire story, being ever so very helpful to even *point out* our hiding place just in case no one believed him to be a victim in our ruthless plot.

To say I am caught with my pants down would be appropriate.

It takes the enraged Tarantula less than a minute to spot my lime greenness skulking behind the banyan tree and less than another minute to land up at our hideout.

'So this is the new low you've stooped to . . . you pathetic little weasels!' Nikita shrieks. 'Trying to poison me so you can go to the dance with my boyfriend? You must be crazy to think he'll even look at someone like you! I'm going to Princi . . .'

Sam breaks in, 'All's fair in love and war dahling, so don't get into a knot over this. Besides, we all know Roberto's been spending time with Angie, so it's only natural that she thinks he's keen on her . . . and BTW it's only a mild laxative not some deadly poison.'

That shut up Tarantula for a moment but I can see Roberto's done with practice and making his way over. All my bravado is starting to fizzle out. It's now or never. I've got to outwit Ms Vakil, scramble up her pea-sized brain a bit in order to get out of this mess!

'It's not about you going to the dance with Roberto. It's whether *he* wants to go to the dance with *you* . . .' I blurt out, my voice shaky and shrill.

'Whaaat? Are you okay?' Nikita looks at me like I'm off my rocker. 'It's the same thing you moron! Roberto and I are a couple, and we're going to the prom together . . . is that clear?'

She was really, really hopping-as-hell mad; given half a chance I'm sure she would have loved to wallop me then and there.

'Not really, you see Angie has a valid point, has Roberto actually *asked* you or are you just *assuming* it because you're allegedly a *couple*?'

Karan's butted in; he's actually a pretty smart fellow despite oodles of moolah, so he's quickly caught on that this might just be his lucky day to win his lady love back if he plays his cards right and finds a legal loophole in dating etiquette.

'What's there not to assume, Karan?' Roberto has turned up, his face guarded and his voice dangerously soft. My heart sinks to the bottom of my shoes. 'What's going on, Nikita?'

'I had absolutely nothing to do with them. Honest, I was forced into putting the laxative in her drink! Angie wants you to take her to the school prom . . . It was Sam's idea . . .'

Venky spills his guts out again in less than a minute and gloriously nails us to the cross.

A deafening silence envelopes the gathering, everyone waiting for the inevitable explosion. My limbs have lost their sensation and all I want to do is throw up.

'You honestly think I was going to ask you to the dance?' Roberto turns on me, his blue eyes blazing ice. Adonis looks bloody scary when angry.

'I thought you liked me . . . my designs . . . all that you said to me at my place . . . during coffee . . .' I mumble desperately through a rising wave of panic.

'You think that because I like your designs that I now have *feelings* for you? Mama Mia! I was only trying to be nice, that's all.'

'Oh Roberto, let the poor thing be, it's hard for Angie as

it is with no looks, no fashion sense . . . . absolutely *nothing* really,' Nikita sighs, sarcasm dripping, her eyes gleaming with victory. And a surge of white-hot rage starts uncoiling from within me. The not-so-nice Angie is waking up, ready to wallop Nikita Vakil once again!

'You poor, poor things trying so hard to fit in with all of us, but I wish you all the best finding a date for the prom dahlings.' Nikki turns; reading the murderous intent in my eyes, slips her arm through Roberto's and walks off, before things get uglier between us.

Sam quickly links her arm through mine and whispers. 'It's going to be all right, Angie. Don't pay attention to Tarantula. I'll sort this out, trust me.'

'I can't believe this girl, Angie . . . how can she even think this? All I was interested was in helping her with the designs . . .' Roberto's voice floats loud on the breeze, stabbing me through the heart.

Sam was right, Roberto is a cad. My eyes are tearing up and my fists curling tightly, eager to punch the living daylights out of Sam and Venky for messing things up for me. For giving me hope that there was and could be *anything* at all with Roberto Missoni.

'Don't let Nikita Vakil get to you, okay?' Karan steps up and awkwardly offers me his CK scented handkerchief. 'Don't lose your confidence.'

I take it gratefully and before I can mumble a snort-free thank you, he's sauntering off, hangdog expression, hands stuffed in his pockets, a lovesick Romeo trying to valiantly put back the pieces of his own torn-up heart. Guess everybody hurts.

* * *

'Oh no, you're not going anywhere, you've got a load of explaining to do Mister Venkatesh Murthy!

A loud pig-like squeal forces me back to the present, back to the ugly debacle that has just occurred. Sam has Venky by the scruff of his neck; spectacles dangling off his nose, eyes bulging with panic . . . it is such a pretty sight!

'Well, well, well. Isn't Venky the perfect friend slayer . . . the bosom pal who simply loves to spill your secrets at the blink of an eye? Thank you so much for thoroughly humiliating me in front of Roberto, I couldn't have asked for more.' I get up real close to the squirming morsel and say each word slowly and deliberately into his face.

'L . . l . . look guys, am really sorry, okay? I was . . . was scared. I'll do whatever . . . whatever you want me to . . .'

'Really Venky? Coz right now I want you to break your own miserable neck!'

'Wait a minute . . . I have a better idea, Angie.' Sam tightens her grip on Venky's neck; her eyes are jumping with excitement. Oh no! Another madcap idea has just gotten hold of her. I'm not listening to her any more. I've been humiliated enough.

'You, Mister Venkatesh Murthy, are going to set things right for Angie; you are going to get none other than Neel Murthy to take her to the prom.'

Neel Murthy! My head reels. He's the blooming Head Boy of Royal International, super intelligent, super drool worthy, a super-duper star!

Sam has truly lost it.

8

BISLY (BUT I STILL LOVE YOU)

But where there's a will, there's a way.

And where there's blackmail, there's an even faster way.

Neel Murthy didn't stand a chance when Sam cornered him at the cafeteria during lunch break the next day and bluntly told him that if he didn't take me to the prom, she would have no option but to tell Venky's Mom, his Akka Sudha, that he smoked! And if there was one person in the world who terrified the hell out of Neel Murthy, it was this particular Akka, the unchallenged matriarch of the Murthy gharana, who had the power to change everyone's fortunes.

Now just imagine, whispered Sam, if Sudha Akka *somehow* caught a whiff of Neel's descent into delinquency—his dream of breaking free from his orthodox parents and fleeing to blonde-filled, action-packed America for his undergrad studies could be ruthlessly and quite unnecessarily squashed with just one phone call . . .

'So it's all set. Neel will pick you up at 7 p.m. He will be your partner for four dances, including the first and the last. All you have to do Angie, is make a really grand entry and knock that Missoni's socks off!'

Sam calls me up later in the evening filling me about the whole episode.

'So make sure your prom dress is the best one ever in the history of Royal International School Proms.'

'You're the bestest bestie ever, Sam! I seriously still can't believe you actually threatened Neel about his smoking and got away with it! Neel Murthy as my prom date, gosh, this is going to be the most awesomest school year ever! Roberto Missoni here I come!' I shriek excitedly, bringing Sulu running into my room and making Cheetos scurry out.

'What happened? Is everything all right?'

'Everything's just absolutely marvellous, Sulu!' I hug my startled granny tightly and pump up the volume on Fergie singing, *There's No Getting Over You*. I grab Sulu and twirl her around, getting her to shake a leg and shimmy to the beats along with me. It's been a long time since I felt so alive!

'Ahhh . . . it's the school prom that's got you all crazy. Look at you all glowing and happy. Well, enjoy the attention of your Italian prince, dahling.' Sulu kisses me on the cheek and walks out closing my door behind her. I stop, struck by lightning.

What on earth am I celebrating about?

That my BF had to blackmail someone to take me to the prom?

Am I so desperate to impress Roberto?

That Neel must break his girlfriend Rhea's heart, tell her he can't dance the two most important dances with her?

What kind of a person am I?

Disgusted, I get up; angrily turn off Fergie and frantically call Sam.

I can't do this!!

'Calm down, Angie, there's no need to panic. You're not committing a blooming murder here, okay?' Sam snaps back. I hear Venky say something in the background that stops her tirade. She giggles hysterically startling me.

'Oh, but that's absolutely fab news Venky! Angie, Angie! Quit hyperventilating . . . Mother of all news . . . Rhea's come down with chickenpox. Yup that's right! Neel told Venky *before* I blackmailed him. So relax, drop the guilt trip and enjoy the attention. Chill okay, I'll be at your place in an hour. It's time we had a sleepover.'

* * *

With less than forty-eight hours left for D-Day evening, my nerves are shot.

I'm soooo stressed that I'm retaining water by the gallons. My face is all puffy, my eyes baggy and my bum saggy. Getting into the slinky number I've created for myself is going to be a tough squeeze if I don't stop ballooning right away.

'Here, drink this. Mom says it works wonders,' Sam hands me a mug of foul-smelling green tea. I HATE green tea! It's odious. I don't care if it has the powers to make me thinner than a rice noodle. Gimme me nice, sweet desi masala chai any day, so what if it's not packed with those fancy antioxidants and whatnots; at least it's got TASTE!

I pretend to sip on the smelly stuff and when Sam's checking her WhatsApp messages, sneakily pour it down the drain.

'Look if that's what you're going to do every time then . . .' I spin around guiltily, spilling the remnants of the tea on to the bathroom floor.

'Oh Sam it's not that, I just don't like green tea, that's all.'

'Neither do I, but it's your only hope now, Angie, if you want to get into THIS.'

She holds up the slinky off-shoulder dress. It's the evening gown created from my sketches for the Teen Runway Contest. The dress is absolutely feline and fantastic, total fashion runway material with its funky black lace peekaboo midriff set against a jungle print camouflage look, held up at the shoulder by a giant black sash that flows all the way down to the floor.

Sam's right.

I make myself a fresh cup of green tea and pull out our pre-prom checklist. Can't have a nail or hair out of place, there's way too much at stake here; we refill our mugs with the necessary fat-burning swill and hunker down going through every detail twice, just to make sure that nothing goes wrong now.

* * *

D-Day! And everything's looking picture perfect.

The every hour green tea, fifty surya namaskaars thrice a day, an hour of the blessed treadmill at incline and no carbs but green salad bootcamp regime works like wicked magic. I can see my cheekbones again, no bags hanging under my eyes and the bottom's perked up big time.

Mom's got Monica, her favourite stylist, to do our make-up and hair. Frankly I have my doubts about Monica's creative skills as everything about Mom—from her hairdos to her make-up to her nail colour—is always soo predictably elegant. But Monica surprises us big time.

Two hours later I am truly transformed into a Full on Fashionista!

My unruly, curly hair has been snipped short at the back leaving long, twisty strands in the front framing my face. Monica then adds a handful of golden highlights making my cheekbones stand out. A splash of metallic bronze on my eyelids, sheer coral lipstick and a touch of light blush and I'm looking like a supermodel!

Sam and I are speechless. We shriek wildly in delight and hug our newfound soul sister. Monica grins, enjoying the attention.

'Wear your dress, let's see the complete look.'

I slip into the dress and much against my wishes; I must pass over my favourite comfortable combat boots for a new pair of black pencil heels that Sam insists I put on. Of course we have our routine BF angry spat with Sam winning thanks to Monica gently pointing out that we're going to a, 'dance party' not a rock show.

I check myself in the mirror for the zillionth time and I really, really like what I see.

It's time to take the world by storm; show everyone what I'm really capable of. Time to go Full on Fashionista!

* * *

Well, Neel Murthy sure did more than a double take when he came to pick me up. He even gallantly offered me his arm as we entered the dance hall with Usher crooning *Baby Tonight DJ Got Us Fallin' Love Again*, the perfect song to my grand, late, but-not-too-late entry.

Tonight I will make heads turn, I tell myself, all pumped up after reading *The Secret*. Tonight is my last chance to make Roberto look at me in a light other than just a coffee buddy.

Sam's grooving away on the dance floor; she's looking rather attractive in a pretty floral dress. No, I haven't designed it; there just wasn't enough time with all this going on. Venky's looking really cool with his slicked back gelled hair and posh formals as he tries to keep pace with Sam's crazy gyrations.

My entry is a ripple effect, like a heavy stone being dropped into a very still and calm pond.

One of Tarantula's minions rushes over to Nikita and Roberto butting in just as he was ready to twirl her. The look on Nikita's face is priceless as she scans me from head to toe taking in my new avatar; disbelief, shock and the dawning realization that she is nearly toast, all play out within seconds. I smile slowly. Roberto's face has incredulity written all over it. He stops dancing, says something to Nikita who now looks ready to explode out of her baby blue Barbie outfit. She's suddenly realized that the spotlight's shifted to me and isn't too happy about it at all.

The ripples have begun to gather strength.

One by one everyone stops dancing and stares. And I mean every . . . single . . . one.

The photographers snap away hungrily, flashbulbs popping like champagne corks, and my head begins to spin lightly. I am on cloud nine. Karan Oberoi pushes through the gawking crowd and walks up to me, a huge grin on his face.

'You're looking awesome, Angie! May I have the next dance with you?'

'You're in the queue buddy.' It's Roberto! My heart starts hammering wildly as I force myself to look into those hypnotic blue eyes.

'Angie, Mia Cara. You look *bellissima*, so very beautiful, like an angel come down from the heavens.'

Everyone's stopped dancing and watching Missoni make his moves. There is no doubt that, I, Angie Kulkarni have captured his attention. For me it's Mission Missoni Accomplished! And then when he suddenly reaches for my hand and gently brushes his lips against my trembling fingers, my knees nearly buckle under!

'Mia Cara Angie, may I have this dance with you?' A knowing smile curls the edges of his lips; he's aware of the crazy effect he's spun on me, so damn sure that I will meekly forgive and forget his earlier unkind words. And it is this arrogance that snaps me out the spell! I pull my fingers out of his grasp, my voice steady and cold.

'Thank you, you look great yourself Roberto. But like you just said, unfortunately you are in the queue *buddy*.' I smile mockingly and turn away, watching him flush red, humiliated.

I am THE STAR of this evening, and I intend to keep it that way.

9

ROFL (ROLLING ON THE FLOOR LAUGHING)

Always watch your back is Mom's mantra.

At this point I am way too busy watching what's happening in front of me—the glorious sight of Roberto and Nikita arguing—that I have no idea what Fate was furiously cooking up behind my back.

The evening so far has been totally AMAZINGLY MAGICAL! Almost everyone, stiff-lipped teachers included, have complimented me on my dress, my hair. 'You look so cool! Fab! Love the outfit; unbelievable you made it yourself! Could you design one for me?' Everyone, except of course Tarantula, who is now making it a point to dance real up close with Roberto right in my face! Roberto's looking a bit uncomfortable with the excessive PDA and is trying to get her to cool off but she's not in the listening mood, at all.

'Ignore him, Angie and he'll come running to you,' says Neel in my ear.

I blush and keep dancing, ignoring Nikki's outrageous behaviour. I try not to think about how I've lost that one chance to dance with Roberto thanks to my stupid, hasty temper.

'Why would you say something so moronic, when you wanted to get him to dance with you in the first place?' Sam gives me an earful when I tell them. 'Honestly Angie, I really don't know what to do with you!'

Exasperated, Sam has stomped off dragging Venky with her to grab a bite. The prom's half an hour away from wrapping up, the DJ slows down the tempo, I scan the dance floor covertly hoping against hope, for another chance, but Roberto's nowhere to be seen, and frighteningly, neither is Tarantula. A sick feeling comes over me just thinking about the two of them together, snuggled up in a corner, whispering and . . .

Neel's cell rings; it's Rhea calling. He excuses himself. I decide to head over to the snack counter all ready to drown my grief in grease when someone grabs my hand.

'I'm jumping the queue if that's all right with you Cara?' Roberto's back!

I can almost hug him in relief. Instead I nod coolly, diva like.

'I'm sorry I said those things, it wasn't right. I really like you, Angie . . . gimme another chance. How about coffee on Monday? You can show me your designs . . . are they ready? The submission deadline is only four weeks away.'

At this moment all I care about is this one person right in front of me. I look up at him and say cheekily, 'So Missoni, do you want to dance or not?'

And I find myself in Roberto's arms as we slow dance, his breath against my hair. I don't say a word, daren't even breathe, in case I'm dreaming all this up. Psychedelic lights flash weaving their spell around us, I'm swept away in happiness when suddenly there's a violent tug at my shoulder; I land on my butt, splattered all over on the dance floor with Roberto standing over me gaping in horror!

People are staring and whipping out their cell phones. What's happened?

And the next thing I know, Neel's charged through the crowd, yanked me to my feet, squashed my bosom roughly to his chest and he's shoving, pushing me off the dance floor towards the back of the hall!

Oh my god, I'm being molested!

It's all happening so fast that my screams are frozen stiff in my throat. Everything's a blur—faces, lights, sounds, as I'm being dragged away to the darkest corner. Suddenly my adrenaline surges in and I let loose a well-deserved kick to Neel's family jewels! He falls to the floor poleaxed, writhing in agony. It's only when he lets go of me that I realize what he had been allegedly groping . . . someone has stepped on the long sash of the bow that holds the front and back of my one-shoulder dress together, ripping it apart . . . OMG! I have had a massive wardrobe malfunction, super big time in front of the *entire* blooming high school! My vital statistics are now possibly WhatsApp posts! I stand there feeling utterly foolish and horrified—Neel had been actually trying to shield me, not grope me.

'Oh my god Neel! I'm sooooooo sorry! I thought you were trying to . . .'

'You're a bloody crazy girl! I could kill you!'

'I know and you should, honestly, I didn't realize that you were trying to help . . .' Once again I am the laughing stock of the school and I burst into a flood of angry tears.

'Hey! It's all right kiddo.' Neel staggers to his feet, grimacing with pain but trying to smile at the same time. 'You've got quite a kick, I must say.'

He's unsure of whether he should comfort me or just let me bawl myself out when Sam barges in and takes charge as always.

'Areey! What on earth happened? Who did this to you? Neel Murthy, you rascal!' And Sam hurls herself at Neel pummelling whatever body parts she can get her fists on. He doubles up in pain once again, making futile attempts to shield himself from her assault. Sam hisses, 'I swear your aunt's going to know more about your rapist tendencies and not just about your smoking!'

'Stop it, Sam! Stop it! Neel hasn't done anything! He's *saved* me, that's what he did.' I yank her away before she pulps up my one and only knight in shining armour. 'Someone out there pulled so hard on the sash that it ripped and my dress fell apart . . .' I break down in shame and begin crying again.

'Look, it's over now. Here, wear my jacket and I'll drop you home.' Neel hands me his blazer, 'I'll be at the entrance.'

'This is no accident; this is deliberate, premeditated . . . . SABOTAGE!' pronounces Sam grandly. 'There is no way the sash would have come undone when snagged on say a chair. It required immense human force to tear it apart.' Sam points to the ripped-up ends triumphantly.

* * *

Did I mention earlier that Sam's a natural legal eagle, that she's determined to become a criminal lawyer, got her heart set on Harvard? Of course, this is just to spite her parents who are keen she follows in their spa therapy footsteps. All that scented massage, meditation nonsense and positive thinking therapy is for old retired folks, me I want to shake up the world—is Sam's stand.

'We must find the perpetrator of this heinous crime. We can't let her get away.' Sam grabs my arm excitedly. But I've had enough of confrontations for the day. I just want to go home. But before I can stop her, Sam's rushed to the DJ's deck, turned off his music and grabbed the mike and unleashed her ire.

'I will hunt down the person who has done this to Angie and trust me, I will sue you for defamation,' yells Sam and points her finger directly at Tarantula.

So now, thanks to my overzealous BF, everyone who *didn't* see what happened will make sure that in the next five seconds they acquire all the gory details. The party's crashed; ground to an uneasy halt, people are looking at both of us with pity and revulsion. I go from being superstar to super loser in one evening, *again*.

'You girls are insane! Why would anyone of us do something stupid like that?'

It's Nikita, high-pitched as usual, making heads turn as she strides up to the console, eyes flashing, her minions following her dutifully. I must admit as much as I hate her, Tarantula does make heads turn. It's the deadly combination of spectacular looks and snooty attitude that puts creatures like her on a different level. She turns to me standing miserably on the fringes, completely vanquished. Her eyes are gleaming, glittering with triumph . . . OMG! She did it! Sam *was* right! But before I can muster up my wits, Nikita goes for my jugular.

'Now why would anyone waste their time trying to mess up Angie's supposedly *amazing* outfit . . . And by the way guys, what exactly *is* it? A costume from Jungle Book meets Dracula?!'

The crowd laughs cruelly, lapping it up. Suddenly, I have this utterly insane urge to throw up on Tarantula when I see Sam rushing down from the console with a stiletto in hand ready to whack her. Light bulbs flash in my face, making me want to scream and lash out in anger, but instead I turn and run out blinded by the rising tide of tears welling up, straight into Roberto's arms . . .

'Hey Angie! Cara, don't let her get to you she's not worth it. You are . . . and I'm over her.' he says tenderly, when at this crucial moment of the roller-coaster evening, Sam's misguided stiletto missile comes flying through the air and lands with unerring precision on Roberto's nose, shattering my brief hope of romance with the only love of my life!

10

NFW! (NO FRIGGING WAY)

Thank god it was the last day of school.

And thank god, Roberto's Italian nose was tougher than Sam's Indian stiletto so all that he ended up with was a very nasty knock and a purple noggin the size of a *chikoo*. As expected, Roberto is now in no mood whatsoever to entertain our apologies and has switched off his cell phone.

'Trust you to fling your stiletto at him! You're way out of control, Sam!'

I just lost it when Sam and Venky dropped by to check up on me.

'Hey don't blame me for everything! Why did you have to go and make a fancy dress with a stupidly extra long sash! Couldn't you have worn something simpler? You know what? I'm sick and tired of bailing you out all the time! Good luck with that design competition and with Mr Missoni the Magnificent. From now on

Geetanjali Kulkarni, you're on your own! Come on Venky, let's go!'

This time I don't stop Sam.

I turn on Lana Del Ray's *Summertime Sadness*, pull out my sketchbook, flop on to my bed and begin to flip through my designs one by one, trying really desperately to forget last night's horrendous nightmare! God, why's this happening to me? Why does nothing ever work out right, just once? Cheetos senses my pain; she leaves her perch and snuggles up against my feet, trying to comfort me.

My cell buzzes, it's a message from Neel, 'Raat gaye baat gaye. Focus on the contest. Talk soon, kiddo.'

He's right. Teen Runway is barely a month away, four weeks to sketch, detail and create three extraordinary outfits . . . I pull out the form hurriedly.

1. Send in your favourite design. Explain the concept and inspiration behind it. Ten contestants from India will be pre-selected on this basis.
2. The selected ten will face the Teen Runway Test in Mumbai. Prepare three designs sketches complete with concept notes: Evening wear, Formal and Casual. Execute and showcase one on the runway.
3. The six Teen Runway finalists will compete in the Grand Finale at the House of Verduce with one week to create their Teen Runway Showstopper.

4. The winner of the Teen Runway Showstopper
   will receive an all-expense paid one year
   internship at the House of Verduce.

The words blur and my mouth suddenly runs dry, 'Oh
god, I'm never going to make it!'

'Well, you're definitely not going to make it if you spend
your time weeping and wailing every time something goes
wrong.'

It's Mom! Didn't realize I was talking to myself. I hurriedly
stuff my sketchbook underneath my pillow and turn around
guiltily. Now, no one except my BFs and Roberto know
about me taking part in the competition. It's my big secret
till right now.

'How was the school prom?' asks Mom, her eyes taking in
my troubled face. 'Angie, is everything all right?' Suddenly
I'm exhausted, I just want Mom to hold me and tell me that
everything is going to be all right. Her voice soft, concerned,
worried, washes over me. It's like childhood times once
again. 'You want to tell me; about it, pilloo?' Her perfume
wafts closer, soothing and comforting. Yes, I want to tell you
everything Mom, get the skeletons out of the closet, and just
let it all out. I take a deep breath and confess everything . . . .

'But that's wonderful pilloo! I'm so proud of you!' Mom
shrieks with delight, jumping up and hugging me. WHAAAT!
Parents sure are crazy. Shouldn't she be like hopping angry
mad 'coz I haven't told her for a good two weeks.

'Now show me your sketches and we'll polish them up.
We can't have you sending in *these* grungy, mangy, grubby

chalta-hai designs. This is a chance of a lifetime. Verduce is all about smooth lines and defined cuts . . . I'll call Suzanne right away, get her opinion.'

And though I know she's right in getting Suzanne aunty's opinion, a sharp pain stabs my heart; Mom still thinks my designs are juvenile *crap*. The all too familiar anger starts uncoiling rapidly, eager to lash out, 'And guess what, Angie? Now that you're taking part in a fashion contest, I have a surprise for you . . .'

'What is it?' I snap back.

'You are coming with me to the Oscars . . .' My heartache catapults into a heart attack!

'All the great designers will be dressing up the stars. Imagine the fashion designs you'll see and get ideas from.'

OMG, she's right, this is an out of this universe opportunity! My anger vanishes and I rush over and give Mom the biggest, hugest bear hug ever.

'You're the sweetest! I love you!' Mom holds me close grinning.

'I know pilloo, so quit moping around, we leave next week. We'll be staying at the Beverly Hills Hotel. And pack light 'coz you and I are going shopping on . . . Rodeo Drive!'

The next day, I sit down with Mom and we carefully fill in the design competition consent form. Surprisingly, Mom insists I send in the rock star inspired design. It's a vibrant fuchsia top, set off by jagged sleeves embellished with studs and get this, a gigantic safety pin at the V neckline! A short, low-slung burgundy skirt over knee-high boots completes this retro look.

By afternoon my abject apologies and persistence on WhatsApp pays off and everyone's back on speaking terms with me. We celebrate my trip with coffee and croissants at our fave haunt, the CCD near my place.

'Don't forget your passport and for heaven's sake don't fall prey to Miley Cyrus's sweet smile and join her in twerking!' warns Sam cheekily making me squirm. Why does my bestie have to say such inane things in front of Roberto? Venky's in his own zone, quietly sipping his coffee blast, looking lost and forlorn. 'Sam's got some valid points, Angie.' Roberto interrupts Sam's running commentary on the dos and don'ts of propah behaviour protocol in Hollywood.

'This is an amazing opportunity. The Oscars Red Carpet is where the world's best designers showcase their most outstanding designs, so try and take pics. But not too obviously as you're walking the Red Carpet too,' is Roberto's sane advice. His nose is still a little puffy but thankfully it's returning to its original magnificent beauty . . . phew! That was a really close call. I shudder remembering that insane incident.

'Gosh, this is going to be so exciting, so crazy. I'm soooo excited for you Angie!' Oh dear, Sam's waving her half-eaten croissant around, oblivious that it may just fly out of her grip and land on the head of the bald fellow at the corner table!

'Well, I'd better get going guys. Loads to do before I leave, I'll call you tomorrow, okay?' I hurriedly get to my feet. Roberto grins and stands up, 'Me too, I must move now. Ciao everyone.'

'Hey, don't forget your mani, pedi, facial, you know the works . . .' yells Sam making everyone in the coffee shop stare at me. I rush out, my face flaming red with embarrassment, and for once I'm quite happy that Roberto's in a hurry to go home.

By the end of the week, I'm all packed and ready to take on Los Angeles, named by the Spaniards as 'The City of Angels'.

* * *

It's really hard being a Bollywood superstar, so even if it's past midnight and half the town's snoring away, you must be photo-shoot ready. Gucci glares, Jimmy Choos, Chanel, not a hair out of place even if you're in jeans 'coz invariably the paparazzi lurks waiting to snap you off guard and then tweet to the whole world about your wrinkles.

Walking the Mumbai Airport with Kajol Kulkarni is like the sea parting for Moses; I love it, and hang on to Mom's hand as we sail through the masses, enjoying the envious stares I get. Of course Mom gets mobbed at every possible stop, and even though we're finally all the way up in first class after having being whisked through security in less than ten minutes, the hysteria continues on flight with passengers sneaking past Prasad, our burly bodyguard, and landing up in our faces!

I have to hand it to Mom; she handles her fame very graciously, signing autographs and posing for the camera with a smile, not an emotion out of place, till her fans are politely but firmly ushered out of first class by the airline staff and we take to the skies. Couple of hours later, over chit-chat, chilled champagne and caviar, Mom discreetly removes her make-up, slips into her track bottoms and dozes off. But me—I don't sleep a wink throughout the flight, I'm all wired up and how!

I flip open my iPad and begin reading the humongous dossier on Hollywood that Sam and Venky have e-mailed me. 'There's SO MUCH to see! And do! Don't just shop okay?' Sam's warned me like a zillion times. I smile evilly and delete her messages, but of course Shopping is FIRST on my agenda. I can't wait to raid Forever 21, Banana Republic and Guess . . . what's this? Never knew there's something called the Walk of Style just like the Walk of Fame! I've gotta see this. I quickly highlight it and mark it down. Excitement mounts as I read on. This unusual sidewalk is a recent addition to Rodeo Drive celebrating the greatest names in fashion like Gianni and Donatella Versace, Manolo Blahnik, and many others . . . wow! What an amazing feeling it must be to be honoured like this!

* * *

We land in the land of Barbie and Ken, where everyone's an actor or a model with bodies to die for, six pack abs and platinum hair, waitressing their way to pay for acting school till they find their big silver screen break la Julia Roberts.

Intimidated by these body beautifuls, I quickly pull in my belly fat, straighten my spine and step out of the airport and do my best to slink into our limo, trying to look like the superstar's super-sensational daughter.

And as we make our way to our hotel, I eagerly soak in the sights of the City of Angels—myriad shapes, sizes, colours and cuts from micro minis to maxis, strappy affairs to sheers, athletic to ascetic, bikinis to bodysuits; from haute couture to grunge, global fashion explodes on these streets with delightful abandon. My heart races with excitement! This is truly the land of freedom; wear what you want without being harassed at the drop of a dupatta. I have closed my eyes and landed in Fashion Paradise!

'Welcome to the Beverly Hills Towers, Ms Kajol Kulkarni. We are honoured to host you. On behalf of the entire staff, may I congratulate you on your much deserved Oscar nomination . . .' the manager greets us, clearly smitten by Mom's elegance. 'As requested, your Paradise Suite overlooks the beach; it has Wi-Fi, a Jacuzzi, a butler on call amongst other deluxe amenities. Do feel free to contact Desiree here at any time.' He introduces Desiree, a smart, petite African American, who flashes a radiant smile at us.

'Please follow me to complete your check-in formalities.' Desiree ushers us over to a cosy lounge. 'I'll have your bags sent to your room.' Tall, cool glasses of Pina Colada appear, and I sip daintily, my eyes peeled hoping to catch a glimpse of these Hollywood celebrities while Mom fills in our check-in details.

The swanky hotel is buzzing with activity. I suddenly choke on my slurp—I've just spotted Johnny Depp, Helena Bonham Carter and Tim Burton deep in conversation at the far end of the café! I love Depp, he's just awesome! And he's the host for the Oscars, beat that! Helena's another favourite of mine with her effortless portrayal of flamboyant, whimsical characters, and what can I say about Burton? He's an absolute genius director! And that's definitely *X Men* Hugh Jackman! Where in the world is Pattinson? Mom! Finish that later, get me an intro, puhleez?! Just then a sudden hush descends and all eyes rise to the scene unfolding before us.

Jennifer Lopez steps out of the hotel lift wearing a white micro sheath that is beyond tiny, leaving very little to the imagination about her fantabulously sculpted body. In comparison, Mom's almost an overdressed mannequin in her chamko desi attire. Lopez greets the now simpering Desiree who has forgotten all about Mom and is scurrying to hold the door open. J Lo breezes past strutting a perfect superstar catwalk to step into her waiting limousine.

Of course there's a crowd waiting to catch a glimpse of J Lo, but apart from the three gawking desis (our poker-faced bodyguard Prasad is now drooling like a hungry dog) the crowd isn't lecherously x-raying her anatomy top to bottom; they're just in plain awe and admiration.

'That's so cheap! Doesn't she realize people are watching her? It's only asking for trouble!' Mom bursts out, muttering angrily in Marathi under her breath, double miffed because none of the desis in that crowd had bothered to mob *her* when she had arrived minutes earlier!

'Mom! How can you say that?' I'm shocked. Honestly, this coming from someone who believes that women should be allowed the same freedom as men. I open my mouth to remind her of the hot pants and bikini shoots of her heydays

when I notice that Lopez's gone, but in her place is . . . .
OMG! My eyes pop out. It's Lady Gaga!

Mom's voice has suddenly faded into the background, the
celebrity pop singer is heading our way, and my heart has
stopped beating. Is this for real? I love Gaga's crazy sense of
fashion, her clothes are indescribable—right now she looks
like she's stepped out of a shredder . . . sooo utterly uber cool!

Okay, we'll debate her fashion sense later, right now I'm
STARSTRUCK. I need a selfie with her, where's my cell
phone? I have precisely five seconds to make the move of a
lifetime when Mom suddenly grabs my arm, pulling me into
the lift just as I've dug out my mobile!

'Mom! Stop it! I want to get a pic.' People are staring
at us, but I couldn't care less. In the blink of an eye, Gaga's
gone, whisked off by her security. I'm hopping mad at Mom
while Ms Kajol Kulkarni, still worked up over being upstaged,
loses her poise and takes it out on poor Prasad.

'Enough of staring, come on! Let's get to our room.
Prasad chalo fetch my bags.' She barks orders, marching into
the elevator and punches the lift button violently, sending us
shooting to our suite.

* * *

An hour later, Mom's calmed down enough to call Dad and
joke about us landing safely in one piece and mercifully with
our luggage intact. Yup, Mom's luggage always goes missing
without fail on all airlines!

'I miss you honey, so much! Yes I promise I won't lose
my temper.'

Mom's a changed person when she's with Dad: softer, nicer when he's around. It's the same with me. I feel safe and carefree, and I chat with him a bit, then blow him a goodnight kiss and hang up. I'm missing Daddy and Sulu and Cheetos, and of course my crazy buddies.

For the next hour as I shower and change, Mom's busy going over her itinerary with her manager Christina D' Cruz and Siddharth Samarth, the director of *Mysterious Maharani*.

'This film will make me immortal,' she had told us when she signed the contract three years ago. Now it all seems to be coming true.

I listen to them, amazed. I honestly didn't think there would be so much action happening! Mom has churned up quite a lot of interest amongst the bigwigs of Hollywood; she's got breakfast, lunch and dinner invitations all week through. There's lunch with Ang Lee, the phenomenal director, breakfast with Danny Boyle and most hugely, dinner with none other than movie Moghul Steven Spielberg!

'Ma'am, you have a dress fitting in forty-five minutes.' Christina gently but firmly interrupts the tense debate about whether the team should accept the Indian Association's last minute puja cum dinner invite tonight.

'Soch lo Kajolji, we really need their support and they've been ek dum first class, marketing our film out here for the Oscar nomination,' pleads Siddharth, his fleshy face troubled, rising heavily to his feet. But it's clear that Mom's not happy with the lukewarm response she's received from the American desi community so far.

'You and the others go ahead; I'll join you if I have the time.' She dismisses Siddharth, her eyes icy, 'Right now I've got to get my Oscar outfit perfect.'

'Please Kajolji, ajao for half hour only please.' He's blubbering now, desperate, 'Look, take the bachchi here to Disneyland, or wherever she wants, it's on the house. Just please ajao tonight, else Mr Jindal will be very upset.'

The doorbell rings interrupting his lament. Christina walks in with the HUGEST bouquet of the most gorgeous white lilies I have ever seen in my life!

'Dekha, see I told you the Indian American Association hasn't forgotten you!' Siddharth laughs nervously, clearly hoping that was the case.

'It's from the Academy Awards Committee,' Mom retorts coldly holding up the gold embossed card. 'Look Sid, I don't do last-minute invites, so leave me out, okay? Tell them I missed my flight.'

'All right, all right, no pressure, just try to come. You have the limo with you, drop in for ten minutes that's all. Do it for the Oscars, theek hain?' And he's finally gone.

'I know we're both dead tired but we'll have to go, just for a bit okay? So grab a shower and pilloo, wear *whatever* you want.' She smiles, ruffling my hair. 'And let's give these guys a taste of true Bollywood ishstyle.' She winks wickedly.

Half an hour later, Kajol Kulkarni steps out looking absolutely smashing superstar, all set to rock the party, like always.

II

ADIP (ANOTHER DAY IN PARADISE)

Sorry to say this, but Desis abroad are stuck in a weird time warp.

It's not like these guys don't have the moolah for housekeeping. They have it all; genius brains, Ivy League credentials, palatial mansions, so what's with the tacky, tasteless metres of plastic sheets covering sofas, carpets, trailing all through your heavenly, humongous mansions and even into your Porsches?

And then there's this really creepy obsession with anything and everything Bollywood. Everyone at last evening's dinner, including the bachcha party, were all togged up to the hilt in the shiniest ghagras and sherwanis quite fit for a wedding! I almost expected them to suddenly get up and burst into a dance or something. Okay I get that you're proud being an Indian and all that but must you go completely overboard trying to prove it?

Predictably, I was underdressed for the do in my ripped Gucci jeans and black Mango T, and so was royally ignored by the chamkchallos who couldn't get enough of posing with Mom. Mercifully the DJ was awesome, the food delicious, the mocktails really funky; and then came the hilarious filmy ending to the evening. Mr Jindal, bolstered by several single malts and completely charmed by Kajol Kulkarni, took the stage and pledged another $ 1,00,000 towards the promotional campaign of *Mysterious Maharani*.

This irked senior Granny Jindal and she totally blew her top. The crabby old lady, who had earlier poked her nose into my plate of pakodas and given me a horrid tongue lashing for wearing phate hua kapde, completely lost her temper! She declared she was done with her family and would now take refuge in Kashi. Ranting aloud, Granny Jindal rushed on to the driveway on her electric wheelchair pursued by her suitably-chastised son begging her to stop, only to topple off into the manicured front lawn, her dentures flying through the air! So this desi party had all the elements of a really happening bash—booze, biryani, bhangra beats and a brawl.

But the evening wasn't a complete loss. I hit it off with the Jindals' youngest, Alisha, a violinist and thankfully she was not into decking up like an Indian Christmas tree. Then there was dishy, suave and funny Imran Khan who was unfortunately Alisha's boyfriend! And so by the time we got home past midnight, we three had discussed, dissected and completely bonded over fashion, music, food, movies, animal rights, and yes the state of our country.

* * *

Kajol Kulkarni is superstar hopping mad.

She's just discovered the notorious neon-black punk rock outfit that gave her a major heart attack at the Movie Mania Awards, as well as the infamous school prom dress that almost killed me, tucked away at the bottom of my suitcase! That's right, I've defied Mom and snuck along the two outfits that I care for the best and Mom hates the most . . .

'I can't believe you brought along these, *these* crazy clothes with you, Angie! There's no way you're turning up for the Oscar dos wearing them. Christina, get the limo, take my credit card and take her shopping. Right now!'

Here we go fashion bashing Angie again . . . I tell myself to control my anger, not say a word, as Mom is now erupting like Mount Vesuvius. Christina rushes out of the room, thoroughly annoyed at having her day messed up.

'Angie, I can't believe you actually think this dress is . . .'

'*Different* . . . I quite like it actually.' Suzanne Singh walks in, all fresh faced and floral in a lovely flowing kaftan. Mom whirls around stunned at seeing her! Astonished myself, I silently thank the gods above for sending the perfect angel to save me.

Suzanne's a gem of a person. Amazing talent and a generous heart, she's mom's dearest associate and the only friend Kajol Kulkarni truly trusts. They've been pals since college, and so Suzanne knows how to handle Mom's diva moments. It's a pity she lives at the other end of town in Mumbai, the travel's way too much for me to just pop over to discuss and debate fashion with her.

'What are you doing *here*?' Mom sputters, anger vanishing, rushing over to Suzanne. 'I thought you were in Paris at the Fashion Week.'

'I was, Kajol, and now I'm here to make sure my friend rules the red carpet.' Suzanne laughs gaily, hugging her back. 'Back to Angie's dress, let's have a closer look, shall we? Let's see if it's red carpet worthy . . .'

She picks up the prom dress and I hold my breath hoping that she doesn't think it's way too different, too radical, thereby convincing me to dump it altogether.

Anxious minutes tick by as both Mom and I wait for her expert verdict.

'Look, I agree that it's not the typical, formal, red carpet type of outfit, but then Angie's fifteen, and she shouldn't be wearing stuffy, predictable, boring *gowns*.' Suzanne smiles and gently tousles my hair. 'Babes, I totally love the jungle look, the clever sash, that midriff is indeed awesome and the fact that's it's a maxi length gives the dress a nice touch of fantasy. With the perfect chandelier earrings and minimal make-up you'll be a showstopper yourself!'

Mom gapes at her best friend in disbelief. 'Suzie, woman are you totally insane?' she protests. 'You've had too much champagne last night, haven't you?'

Me? I'm totally over the moon! This is huge! Compliments from an award-winning, much-sought-after fashion designer——I'm so thrilled I'm grinning widely, infuriating Mom even more.

'This is not Bollywood, Suzanne, where kuch bhi chalta hai, okay? This is Hollywood, the Academy Awards, the Oscars . . .' Mom's going red in the face.

'I know, Kajol. Don't get so worked up, just chill yaar and let Angie have some fun. Why not give her a chance to wear her own creation? It's actually very interesting. And anyway, everyone's going to be looking at *you* Kajol, you're our star tonight. So come on, we need to get started on you, there's very little time; hope you've got your Oscar speech ready,' Suzanne gives me a sly wink. 'And you young lady, better run along for your spa appointment.'

I quickly scoop up my dress and walk out of the room, silently thanking Suzanne aunty for stepping in before things got out of hand.

* * *

No one can take their eyes off Kajol Kulkarni.

She is the Mysterious Maharani: autocratic, regal, divine, sexy and ethereal in the gorgeous turquoise Paithani half sari worn over a black satin petticoat topped with a long-sleeved, backless, silver brocade choli. Her tied hair carelessly cascading down her slender back, dark kohl-rimmed eyes contrasting against those luscious red lips. Her only piece of adornment are these gigantic earrings made out of the traditional Maharashtrian nose ring, the nath.

Kajol glides out of the limo taking her time to live the moment. She is so different from the Hollywood divas desperately working their best angles with the paparazzi. Mom allows her vulnerabilities to show just enough to silently rule the hotly contested red carpet. It is a riot, the crowds, the paparazzi; they just love the exotic Indian actress who is all set to change the rules of the game. And guess what? I am doing pretty well myself too. There was one photographer who just kept following me all the way up the red carpet into the foyer! And I even had some people ask for my autograph!

We make our way smiling, waving, and signing through a storm of flashing cameras and screaming fans up the grand staircase, into the magnificent, plush Dolby Theatre. We sit down next to Siddharth and suddenly I'm aware that this is the final countdown. I reach out and clasp Mom's hand. She squeezes it back, and I sense her nervousness underneath the cool mask.

'Oscar humara hain,' I whisper. 'Lock kiya jaye.'

Mom smiles back gratefully, taking a deep breath to calm herself. The LA Philharmonic Orchestra strikes up signalling the start of the much anticipated Academy Awards. People rustle their silks, satins and tuxedoes quickly settling down in their seats. Music rises into the air for the crescendo sending a frisson of excitement through the gathering. At this point a familiar figure strides on to the stage wearing a huge top hat and my heart sings with joy—it's Johnny Depp, the host for the evening! I remind myself to try and acquire his autograph and pic later this evening. Oh this is so amazing! How I wish Sam, Venky and Roberto were here with me tonight. I miss them so!

For the next three hours I sit in an absolute trance wowed over by the sheer magnitude and magnificence of the event. Everything is so skilfully and professionally performed. The aerialists and fire spinners put on a spectacular show, and even the unpredictable Lady Gaga controls her wild side and charms everyone with her latest hit!

The tension is palpable now as the more popular and well-known categories come up for grabs. They've saved the best for the finale. The Achievement in Directing has just been awarded to Tim Burton. Finally his genius is acknowledged! Burton delivers an eloquent speech that gets everyone a bit teary eyed, especially me.

'We now come to the nominees in the category of Performance by an Actress in a Leading Role . . .'

I'm so wired up; I've dug my nails into the armrest.

Mom and Siddharth are simply frozen, expressionless; waiting . . . the movie's three-minute-clip flickers on to the screen ending with a thunderous round of applause.

'Those, ladies and gentlemen, were the five nominees for Performance by an Actress in a Leading Role . . .' Mom's hands are clasped in prayer, her eyes shut. It's now or never. 'And the Oscar for best actress goes to . . . .'

Depp is opening the envelope. I can't contain myself and scream 'Kajol Kulkarni Jai Ho!' almost drowning out his words.

'. . . In the movie *Mysterious Maharani*.' He finishes my sentence.

It's happened! Mom's won! I fling myself happily at Mom. Elated, Siddharth jumps up, pumping the air with his fists. Everyone is standing and applauding. Mom looks like a deer caught in the headlights: scared, terrified, ready to bolt.

'Ladies and gentlemen, please welcome the exquisite Kajol Kulkarni from Bollywood India.'

Mom grabs my hand and gives it a tight squeeze before she makes her way to take her place amongst the stars.

12

POV (POINT OF VIEW)

Thirteen missed calls from Sam!

Oh boy, she's going to make kheemapav out of me! I've been meaning to ring her but everything's been happening so fast, I can barely breathe.

'Hey Sam, how are you? Sorry yaar, been soooo busy . . . no, no, haven't forgotten you guys at all, the Oscars were awesome. Guess you know, Mom won! Totally amazing, yes, and you're not going to believe the people I've met . . .' Sam listens breathless, all agog with excitement as I fill her in with all the juicy news when there's an incoming call. It's Roberto!

'Angie, you're not going to believe what happened at school . . . it's outrageous!' Sam launches into another story but I'm no longer listening, Roberto's trying to get through, I've got to cut Sam short. Right now.

'I'll get back to you Sam, gotta go . . .'. I switch calls, my heart beating wildly.

'Hey Cara, wassup? How were the Oscars?' Roberto's voice floats down the line making me tingle with happiness.

Why haven't you been answering my messages, I almost burst out, what's kept you so busy? But instead I speak coolly, making sure my voice sounds husky and alluring.

'Oh, the Oscars were amazing! And the red carpet was a live fashion runway . . . with simply out of the world, eye-popping designs. It was just super! I've got some stunning pics of my favourites.'

'Yeah, my aunt told me that this year they've dressed many of the celebrities . . .' I note that he makes no attempt to explain why he hasn't called back.

'So what's been happening with you Roberto? You seem to be quite busy, not answering my messages.' There, I have thrown caution to the wind and addressed the issue.

'Well, there's something we need to talk about . . . when do you get back?' My heart plummets, oh no! What's happened? Are he and Nikita going out again? Is he still mad at Sam for knocking up his nose?

'Sure Roberto, I'm back in Mumbai the day after tomorrow.'

'Great. Come over to my place then. I've gotta go now, I'll see you then ok, Ciao!' He disconnects in a rush. I'm left wondering what on earth is going on here and as a result clean forget to call my bestie back.

* * *

'Geetaaanjali! Come on pilloo! Get ready quick, limo arrives in fifteen minutes, time to check out the City of Angels.'

Mom's been really trying hard; actually listening to me like never before, making sure she's not being judgemental when voicing her opinions. The three of us—Suzanne, Mom and I—are heading out to Rodeo Drive this morning for a daylong shopping spree; we leave the day after for India and want to make sure we don't miss out on the headiest part of the Hollywood experience. So ganjis, shorts, sunscreen, credit cards, and we're off on a whirlwind tour of LA. We've picked our favourites, the famous 'must photograph' Hollywood sign which towers over the valley, the Walk of Fame, a sidewalk no movie buff should miss; betcha Mom's name is going to be there soon. Next up is the Walk of Style which honours iconic fashion designers (my name too shall be there one day!) and of course the celebrated Rodeo Drive, where the world's finest designers flaunt their latest collections fresh off the runways.

The afternoon flies by lifting my dark mood a wee bit as we window shop and banter like crazy over our favourites, mine being of course—Guess, Gap and Versace.

'The art lies in the detailing. The more precise and exact you are in your design, the more striking it becomes. That is the secret of timelessness.' Mom points to the exquisite Chanel dress she's picked out in the store.

'But Mom, fashion isn't always about being eternal and timeless. Most labels are so PREDICTABLE like they are made for old, stuffy people! Fashion for me is being adventurous, being with the *times*!' I blurt out loudly getting heads to turn.

Suddenly Mom turns a ghastly putrid colour. What's happening? I turn around and come face-to-face with the very tall and very angry Jadis, the White Witch of Narnia, the contender whom Mom had just beaten to win the Oscar for Best Actress!

'I'm so sorry Tilda! My daughter didn't really mean what she said.'

What's Mom babbling away apologizing to *her* for? You're the Oscar lady babes!

Mercifully, Mom suddenly seems to recall that she, the Bollywood actress, has beaten this high-powered Hollywood artist to the Oscar! She effortlessly switches to superstar mode.

'Angie, this is Tilda Swindon. She's also the brand ambassador of my favourite designer line, Chanel.' And very, ever so casually Mom makes sure her bag bearing the same brand logo is visible as she shakes Tilda's hand.

My tube lights suddenly turn on . . . OMG! Now I remember reading that *Vogue* interview of Tilda Swinton, better known to us teens as Jadis the White Witch of Narnia, being chosen as Chanel's new face!

But Jadis isn't buying into mom's friendly gestures. My legs have turned to jelly and I wait for her strike me dead when suddenly the White Witch calls out imperiously, 'Karl, come here, hurry!'

This is getting completely out of hand. Maybe we've stepped into a time portal and landed up in modern-day Narnia! I look around absolutely terrified, half expecting that horrid looking evil dwarf slave to pop up from behind the racks with a box of Turkish delight to tempt and capture me!

Footsteps clatter closer, I hold my breath and find myself looking at none other than the formidable, ponytailed fashion legend, Karl Lagerfeld!

'Karl, this . . . this *child* here has something very interesting to say about your new Chanel collection.' Tilda's voice drips venom.

This is going from bad to really, really worse. Why do people listen into other's conversations? It should be against the law; you can't just go around eavesdropping, what ever happened to freedom of speech huh? At this point, Mom's as stumped as I am, wondering how best to handle Tilda and her tirade.

'The child finds labels boring, made for stuffy, old people. Am I correct?' At that, Karl's dark glasses pin me down like a cockroach being dissected in lab class.

'Hi, I'm Kajol Kulkarni from India. I'm an actress and I love your collections . . .' Mom pipes up trying to distract Karl from actually dissecting me. 'I'm definitely picking up your absolutely divine dress here . . .' she grabs the outfit we had just been critiquing!

'We all love your collections Karl; I especially adored the Paris Bombay one, so divine, except one can't really wear *tweed* in Indian weather . . .'

Thank heavens it's Suzanne aunty. She had popped over to the next store to discuss the possibility of them stocking her latest collection. Mercifully she has made it back in the nick of time to save our skins.

'I'm Suzanne Singh, fashion designer from India and this young rebel is Angie. She dreams of being a fashion designer some day.'

'Really? So Angie didn't *you* find my Paris Bombay collection *boring*? Old, outdated? Ja?' he growls menacingly.

Hey Bhagwan, why can't I just keep my opinions to myself?

'Ermm . . . well, the truth is . . .' I begin nervously.

Say it Angie! Spit it out! I hear Sam's voice urging me; it's now or never; so say what you truly feel. That it was a tad too stuffy for you? Doesn't matter what he thinks . . . So I close my eyes, take a deep breath, clear my head, remember my elocution classes, and hope for the best.

'With all due respect Sir Karl and Ma'am Tilda, we all know that fashion is not only about haute couture and trends and threads, but also about connecting with one's inner voice.'

Mom's jaw drops to the floor. She can't believe that I can think, let alone say something so deep and profound. But suddenly I'm no longer afraid of what others think of my opinions, I continue recklessly. Suzanne smiles and winks at me. Go on kiddoo, it's now or never, says her expression.

'I'm an aspiring designer; and wore my own creation to the award ceremony because I wanted to be ME—the rebel and yet shy, so I created the outfit in both lace and camouflage print chiffon.'

'That was you? It was such an incredible dress!' Tilda suddenly smiles delighted. 'You liked it too Karl, remember when we were looking at the *Vanity Fair* pics you said it was radical and young.'

Karl reluctantly acknowledges her with a wave of his gloved hand. White Witch has thawed, ice broken, she clasps my hand in a warm handshake, 'Bravo little one! That dress was amazing. You have one spunky, talented brat, Kajol. Cherish her.'

Mom's so relieved; she quickly recovers with a gracious smile.

'Thank you and we do deeply apologize, Angie honestly didn't mean to offend you. It's just that she's always been an outspoken kid. So could we please buy you coffee?'

'Yes, I want to talk to zhis kid of yours some more. Maybe I'm missing something ja?'

We spend the next hour sipping cappuccinos, nibbling delicious biscotti while Karl nurses his Diet Coke and grills us on everything that's latest in India—politics, religion, Bollywood and its hip-thrusting item numbers and of course, the India inspired fashion trends which have taken international runways by storm.

'Zee fashion world is brutal, everyone has talent by zee suitcases, what you will need most is a pair of hard-working hands and an iron heart,' Karl rasps when I quizzed him on being successful. 'Only zhen will you ever be a legend.'

I sit glued to my seat, soaking in every word they're discussing, how collections are conceptualized, what makes them runway successes, how to think out of the box and find inspiration . . . it's absolutely exhilarating. I frantically take notes on my phone as the sun sets a bit too soon on this wonderful evening.

Our bags are packed and we're on our way home.

I'm so wired up, totally hating the insanely long flight. I just can't wait to meet my friends; Sam's already fixed up a sleep over the day after at her place when I remember Roberto's curt message 'C ya soon. Call me.' And I start to worry again.

What *does* he want to talk to me about?

Sam's predictably unreachable or rather chooses to be. But her I can always manao. It's Roberto that worries me. Something is seriously, majorly wrong, and I'm beyond terrified. I try distracting myself by reading a couple of fashion magazines but to no avail.

'It'll blow over pillo, trust me, whatever it is you need to just ride it out. I'm sure it's nothing, so just chill . . .' Mom touches my cheek. Oh, how I wish I could believe her!

13

ILU (I LOVE YOU!)

I've turned up at Roberto's doorstep a couple of hours after landing in Mumbai, seriously jet-lagged and scrambled brained but no amount of Mom's reasoning can convince me to wait till the afternoon. And I'm determined to look absolutely drop-dead chic for this meeting so instead of my usual ultra-casual outfits, I've picked a Forever Young floral halter over white Gap capris, Nine West open toes, hair tamed and tied in a loose ponytail with just a smidgen of barely there make-up, very European, hoping the vision of the new elegant me makes Roberto Missoni think ten times about hanging out once again with Tarantula.

'Hi, come on in Mia Cara Angie.'

He's looking Adonis as ever, all lean and bronzed in a white T over jeans; I flash him a bright smile, quickly suck in my America returned desi paunch and follow him into the living room. And there I get the shock of my life!

There's Tarantula sitting on the couch, sullenly leafing through a magazine. She's is the last person on earth that I want to meet right now!

'What's going on, Roberto? What's *she* doing here?' I blurt out as a sick feeling begins to uncoil from deep within, gripping my stomach in a knot of revulsion.

'Nikita wants to talk to you,' Roberto says. 'Come sit down Angie, you guys need to sort things out.' And the knot in my stomach gets tighter.

Nikita looks up at me, and grins evilly, she's noted the terror in my voice and she's thrilled.

'*What's going on, Roberto? Roberto thinks I should take part in this contest. What do you think of this design, Roberto?*' she mimics, mocking me.

'What's wrong with you, Nikita?' I lash out angrily thinking, does this woman like getting smacked around?

All of a sudden, she angrily flings the magazine aside and jumps up, shouting in my face. 'I'll tell you what's wrong Miss Geetanjali Kulkarni . . . You are! That's what! Pretending to be oh-so-different from all of us but you can't fool me with your so-called talent for fashion designing! You have no fashion sense whatsoever. Taking part in the Verduce Contest . . . blah! Oh, I know what your design label should be called . . .' and she gestures laughing maniacally, 'Teens . . . Run . . . Away!'

'That's enough Nikki!' Roberto grabs her arm, pulling her away from me before I react and lash out. 'You told me you wanted to apologize to Angie for what happened at school and at the prom so that's why I invited you both home. So you could patch things up, not this . . .' Roberto's handsome face is flushed with anger, his blue eyes icy with rage.

'Well guess what, Roberto Missoni? I lied! I have no intentions of apologizing to a two-bit Wannabe Fashionista whose mother is a lousy actress with . . . betcha Angie doesn't know this . . . a really shady past!' Nikita sneers triumphantly watching the colour drain from my face.

'Scusi! That's enough! I'm afraid you must leave my house.' A stern voice interrupts, cutting through the wild tempest of thoughts that are now creating havoc within me What did she just say? *An actress with a shady past?* What on earth is Nikita talking about? I whirl around confused and bump into the statuesque Mrs Isabella Missoni.

'Kajol is a very, very talented actress and you, young lady should watch your tongue. Roberto *Idiota!* Be very careful who you bring into our home.' She stares down at Tarantula who glowers at her with hatred.

'Laxman! Idhar aao please.' A strapping Maratha appears from the wings. 'Madam ko darwaza dekhao please.'

Laxman frog-marches the irate Nikita Vakil out of the Missoni house like a goonda from a Bollywood flick but the comic moment is wasted on me as I'm reeling with shock.

'Sit down Cara, here, have a drink,' Isabella holds my trembling hand and leads me to the couch. Roberto fetches me a glass of chilled Coke, his eyes worried. He glances at his mom. She says something in Italian, I cannot understand.

'Will someone please tell me what's going on here? What's all this about my mother's past?'

'Roberto will tell you what he knows.' Isabella avoids my eyes. 'Angie, please excuse me, I have an appointment with the dentist now, but do come visit us again Cara. And don't worry, all will be okay, si?' she smiles nervously and leaves us in awkward silence. I force myself to take a sip of the drink, telling myself, just like Mom believes, that nothing on earth can be so bad to stress over forever. But Roberto's next words send my world spinning . . .

'It seems that a few days ago, Nikita's Mom, Ramona Vakil who is the anchor head of Starry News Channel, received an anonymous e-mail claiming that your mother had been married earlier. Nikita said the channel is thinking about running the scoop.'

'Whaat!' I jump up in fright. 'But that's insane! Impossible! Look, am sure my Mom's dated several guys before she met Dad, and that each one wanted *her* to marry him but *Dad* was the one she fell in love with . . . This is utterly ridiculous! I've seen the wedding video and photos; they've been together for sixteen years!' I began frantically dialling Mom when Roberto puts a hand on my arm to stop me. I continue angrily, 'Ramona's always been after us, even at the Movie Mania Awards, she made fun of me, called me a Wannabe Fashionista!' I still can't forget that dreadful night.

'Look Angie, you know what Nikita's like. Maybe she's made this up. Don't panic, am sure it's nothing, just some crazy fan trying to get your Mom's attention . . . you know how people love sensational stuff about film stars . . . and am sure Nikita's Mom will cross-check the source before running something like this.'

I stop trying to call Mom. Yeah, Roberto's probably right, like that lovesick fan who threatened to kill himself if Mom didn't cast him in her movie. Or the time when Mom had put on weight for a role two years ago; her rivals insinuated she was pregnant! Why now I remember, Ramona had been the first to air that rumour. But somehow this time my gut feeling isn't one hundred percent sure that this is only a gimmick.

'Am sure it's just idle gossip. Besides, so what if she was married earlier?' Roberto says softly.

'Of course there's nothing wrong, but still she would have told me . . .'

'You don't have to tell everyone *everything*, Mia Cara . . .'

'I'm not just anyone, I'm her only daughter and she's my mother. Why didn't she tell me this? Doesn't she trust me?"

'Maybe she was waiting for the right time. Look I know this is shocking and you have a lot of questions to ask her. Just be calm and if you want to talk about it, I'm there for you . . .'

Roberto leans over and gently takes my hand in his.

I go from shock to ultra-shock state in a nanosecond. I will drown in those blue eyes. Waves of desire begin to rise along my skin, sending my heart racing. So this is what love feels like! I'm breathless, my eyes pull away from his and come to rest on his neck where his pulse pounds furiously. I'm in a trance and before I know it, three words tumble out of my mouth with a life of their own.

'Is this true what you just said, that you love me?' his breath flutters against my cheek. I can feel his heart thumping like a thousand drums, his arms tighten around me, breathing is a serious issue now and so I'm now declaring my passion for him to his neck.

'Yes, Roberto. I do.' This is it . . . I close my eyes waiting for the moment to surrender my soul when my cell pings, interrupting the magic; I've got mail, and it's from Teen Runway!

* * *

I promptly have a heart attack of a different kind.

'I'm one of the ten selected! Woo hoo!' I shout and fling myself into Roberto's arms and before he knows it, I have kissed him smack on the lips quite energetically. He's so stunned, he sits frozen, unsure of how to respond to *me* molesting *him*, and it's quite funny till the impulsiveness of the moment changes its shades.

Roberto laughs gently cupping my face in his hands and whispers, 'Mia Cara Angie, you are one crazy girl.'

You're telling me? But I have no voice. I just look into those eyes and I know that this is where I want to be, in his arms, forever.

* * *

This time I tell my BFs all.

Sam's eyes pop out in shock; Venky gasps and almost

chokes on the vadapav Chotu's served us as I begin to narrate Nikita's melodramatic nonsense.

'How dare she say that about Kajol aunty! I should have been there, would have bashed her in!' says Sam violently waving her vadapav around like a weapon.

'Call up your Mom right now and warn her Angie,' interrupts Venky. 'She needs to know.'

But where on earth *is* Mom? I'm dying to share my greatest news with her. And to ask her about the rumour as well . . .

It's late in the evening, and neither Mom nor Sulu are answering their cell phones. What is going on?

'Go on, and then what happened when Tarantula was thrown out?' Sam asks impatiently.

I force myself to stop worrying about Mom and show them the e-mail on my phone.

'I have made it to the top ten Teen Runway contestants from India!' Saying it aloud makes it so much more real.

'Congo gurl! Way to go! We knew you'd get selected!' They are so happy for me it's huge bear hugs and high fives for a good three minutes. 'Come on Venky, we'd better go, Angie's got to get moving on her sketches and we've got homework to finish unlike someone who's going to be a famous fashion designer.' Sam grins, teasing me. She's now getting to her feet.

'Wait! There's more . . .' I can't hold back my biggest secret any longer . . .

'Then you whaat? I can't believe you KISSED him!' Sam shrieks wildly in total disbelief. Venky's has got the most peculiar look on his face: anger, incredulity and despair; it's a maniacal Dexter Venky I've never seen before.

'And then what happened? Did he say anything? Do anything? What was it like? Come on tell us!' Sam fires a volley of questions.

'Nothing major happened, Sam . . .' I mumble suddenly clamming up, not wanting to share any more. It's honestly way TMI [Too much information]; so I say, 'Really, just a buddy kiss, that's all.'

'Baby memsahib! Jaldi aao, see this!' Chotu is banging frantically at my door. We all rush out wondering what's happened. 'Dekho! Look.' he points to the television screen. 'Memsahib again TV pe hai.' He grins and squats down to read the Hindi subtitles. Chotu loves every bit of Bollywood news, and when it's about Mom, it's a must see. He is one of Mom's biggest fans.

* * *

It's Starry News Channel. There's Ramona Vakil, Mom *and* Sulu in the studio! A chill runs down my spine; Roberto's warning has come true—Ramona Vakil's got her channel to lure Mom into a trap! Mom's cell's switched off, drat it! How do I warn her? Venky grabs the remote and turns up the volume.

'Today's debate is "Stars and Marriages". I would like to warmly welcome to the Starry News Channel studio India's most celebrated actress Kajol Kulkarni who has just won the

Oscar for Leading Actress. With her is Kajolji's mother, the critically acclaimed artist, Soluchona Saxena.'

Ramona Vakil is best described as a skinny, anorexic adult stuck in her twenties, botoxed, tummy tucked and salad fed to fit into her daughter's jeans with a fashion sense that can only be described as—this Devil shouldn't wear Prada!

'Oops . . . praying mantis begins speech, save us!' giggles Sam; making me smile and Venky roll his eyes.

We all remember the day Ramona had been invited to the school as a guest speaker during the Career Forum Week. Even Princi had become rather annoyed with Ramona bragging on and on about her holier-than-thou values and ethics. It was clear from my spats with Nikita that the Vakil gene pool was a judgemental lot and the all-too-familiar knot of fear begins to uncoil, rising up, seizing my innards, twisting them so can I hardly breathe. For the first time, I'm afraid for Mom.

'Now, we Indians are great admirers and followers of this sacred institution that we call *marriage*. Which many of us believe should be a long-lasting bond that is not to be taken lightly, just like our parents did, right?' Ramona asks, smiling sweetly at them.

Mom nods slightly, hesitant, trying her best to look calm and composed but I can detect the tension lurking just beneath the surface of her skin. She's sensed the danger but doesn't know the magnitude of what's heading her way. Sulu, on the other hand, looks relaxed and unconcerned.

'Kajol, you have a lovely family and you've been married

for about sixteen years, am I correct? I believe that our daughters go to the same school. That's sooo charming, isn't it?' Ramona's sweet talk is beginning to alarm me big time. 'So you won't mind if I ask you a very personal question?' A second later, she drops the explosive, 'Kajolji, were you ever married to a Denise D'Souza?'

Mom is so stunned that her superb acting skills fail her completely. Before she can recover her composure, her expression has said it all.

'I err . . . I was very young, only eighteen, in love but he was just . . . I had to get out because . . .' Mom valiantly struggles with the surge of forgotten pain and demons long dead and buried.

'Because of *what* Kajolji? Denise D' Souza was the love of your life, you ran away with him, got married in a temple, but then just months later you walked out of the marriage, taking every single thing with you—even the cat!' Ramona shakes her head sadly. 'Totally shattered by this heartless desertion, ladies and gentlemen, the once-famous photographer Denis D'Souza today is a broken man . . .'

The picture of a grimy, sour-faced man flashes across the screen. Mom winces and shudders. Chotu's eyes are the size of footballs; he's glued to every word scrolling at the bottom of the screen. Clearly, he hadn't expected this turn of events.

'Look, yes I did love him . . . I did run away and get married but . . . soon after that . . .'

'Here's what actually happened.' Ramona interrupts rudely pointing her finger at Mom, not allowing her to finish.

'Soon after that you met film director Vikas Rai, who offered you the lead role in his film. But you knew that if Rai found out you were married, he would drop you like a hot potato and your starry dreams would be killed forever. So you found the perfect legal loophole—that a temple marriage between a Hindu and non-Hindu is invalid . . .' Ramona leans back triumphantly, allowing the implication of her words to sink in. 'And decided to dump Denise right away . . .' She's made Mom look like such a scheming, heartless person!

'Your fans, the entire nation, wants to know, why did you, Ms Kajol Kulkarni, keep this marriage a secret? What else is the famous Ms Kajol Kulkarni hiding from all of us? And is her mother Ms Sulochana Saxena helping her to cover those secrets? We are asking for answers please . . .'

Now, never, ever bait a superstar, especially a superstar's mother. And Ramona had been arrogantly foolish enough to do just that.

'This is totally absurd! You are completely overstepping limits Ms Vakil. Kajol isn't hiding anything from people. Neither is she answerable to anyone. Frankly it's none of your business. If this absurd, unwarranted character assassination doesn't stop right here, right now, I'm going to sue you and your channel for defamation!'

My heart leaps with joy. At last, it is Sulu now morphed into the formidable Sulochana Saxena avatar, pepper-and-salt hair askew, eyes blazing. She cuts the vicious Vakil off in mid-oration.

'Way to go Sulu!' Sam jumps up with joy, hugging Venky,

squashing his spectacles. 'Man, she's some granny, wish she was mine!'

'I'm sorry; I didn't mean to offend you Ms Saxena. I believe you've been through *three* marriages . . . Kajolji must have got all that expert advice on how to go through her divorce from you.' Ramona snipes viciously, not ready to back off just yet.

Sulu is frothing at the mouth ready to throttle the spiteful Ramona, when Mom reaches out for her hand in a calming gesture.

'Yes, of course my mother helped me. But let me tell everyone once and for all, what *really* happened Ramona dahling . . .'

Woo hoo! Mom's famous temper's back! She's ready to kick that nasty Vakil's skinny butt on national television.

'This is going to be good!' Sam grins wickedly.

'I never wanted to leave Denise D'Souza; I loved him too much even though I knew he drank and gambled. My mother warned me but I didn't listen; love does that to you. Within days of getting married, Denise began harassing me for money. When I refused to ask my mother, he bashed me up and threw me out; I spent the day on Chowpatty Beach wondering what to do when Rai Sahib and his family happened to stop by for paanipuris. They noticed me and we struck up a conversation. Meeting Rai Sahib changed my life. He insisted that I audition for his film even though I was married. Now what you *don't* know is that I went *back* to Denise D'Souza, after a week, because I still loved him, believing things would change. They never did. Abuse followed by apology soon became a regular affair. Anything, a random phone call or a silly overcooked dish, would trigger violence. Finally I had enough. I left before he could hurt me any more. And I signed the film a month *after* the divorce.' Mom's voice is flat, cold and hard, her eyes glitter with fury.

'But you could have tried to stay on and work things out instead of deserting the poor man for a filmi career, after all he was your husband . . . and marriage is not a joke in our country,' interrupted Ramona self-righteously, still trying to rattle Mom.

'But I'm really surprised at *you*, Ms Ramona Vakil,' Sulu breaks in. 'You have a daughter, right? Is this the stance you'd take if, god forbid, the same thing happened to her? That as a mother, as a parent you'd just sacrifice your child because of what society says, allow her to be humiliated, tortured . . .' Sulu unleashed her ire, deftly turning the tables on the nasty woman.

Ramona went pale, two red spots of fury popped up on her skinny cheeks, she was furious!

'There is no need to bring my daughter into this!'

'Absolutely! Just like there was no need for you to bring *my daughter* on to your show and try to defame her.' Sulu's eyes blaze with fury.

Sam and Venky grab my hands; we're all glued to the melodramatic turn of events unfolding on national television.

Mom has by now recovered her composure; she leans across and touches Sulu on the arm, signalling her to calm down. But Sulu's had enough. Her voice rises angrily.

'Kajol maybe is a superstar but she's first and foremost *my* daughter and anyone who dares hurt her must deal with me, her mother, first!' Sulu gets to her feet imperiously. 'Ms Ramona Vakil, thank you so much for hosting us. You'll be hearing from our lawyers tomorrow morning. Good night!'

* * *

We didn't even notice Dad come in till Chotu catches sight of sahib's shoes and lets loose an ear-splitting shriek that freaks everyone out. Dad is cool as a cucumber, listening to us calmly but we all know he is seething with rage. Sam and Venky hurry home soon after, Dad and I wait for the irate ladies to return home. But dinner is the last thing on their minds.

It's gotten really late by the time Sulu gets off the phone with her solicitors, making sure that Ramona Vakil will wake up to a slew of legal notices.

I seize the first lull in the storm and bombard my mother, 'Mom, why didn't you tell me about this? Why did you hide it from me? Don't you trust me?'

'She didn't hide it from you deliberately, Angie,' Sulu speaks up, her eyes weary. 'Kajol just wanted to forget and start afresh. It just wasn't that important.'

'This? And not important? Please Sulu, I'm a teenager, not a kid!'

'No, you're definitely not a child, my pilloo.' Mom comes over and holds me tight, 'Of course I trust you but what I did . . . walking out on someone dear to me is not something I'm proud of. But I had to escape . . . .' Her face clouds over with immense sadness. I see that in spite of the pain he caused her, she still mourns for her first love. Suddenly I'm angry at Denis D' Souza, at Ramona Vakil and at all those bullies who expect you to put up with abuse of any kind!

'There's more to a relationship than just passion. It is respect for each other. That's what life is all about,' says Dad brusquely. I see the love shining in Dad's eyes, for Mom, for me and for Sulu. And I'm blown away by the intensity of his emotions. All my doubts and fears vanish.

'Make a wish pilloo,' Mom whispers breaking into my thoughts. She points to a shooting star streaking across the midnight skies. 'Mine came true,' she smiles and goes up to stand close to Dad. He smiles back and gently kisses her forehead. It's the perfect moment to share my great news.

'Top ten in India! Wow! My pilloo the Full On Fashionista!' Dad rushes to pop his best champagne. It bubbles over, like our happiness.

'May all your dreams come true,' beams Sulu taking a sip. 'Especially the crazy ones!'

14

GAL (GET A LIFE)

Each day brings you closer to the truth.

I march into Royal International School ready to face my demons with my angels by my side and this time the show of solidarity isn't only for me. A tiny, but very important detail that Nikita Vakil ignored when she spotted me and decided to take a good panga at me as revenge for her mom getting into a legal mess.

Twenty minutes to assembly and her loud voice cuts all the way across the quadrangle where I'm hanging with Sam and Venky. 'You guys know my aunty Anna who lives in Beverley Hills na? The one—jiska million dollar mansion is right next to Jennifer Anniston's?'

Hey Bhagwan! This aunty of hers seems to live in a mobile home that goes cross country, London, Kiev, Istanbul, Sydney, even Sudan! She always seems to be on the move depending on where Tarantula wants her to go!

'She was at the Oscars and she told my mom that it was all rigged you know, like match-fixing . . .' Her minions gasp on cue and all those pretty little liars turn to look straight at me, baiting me, waiting for me to lose it.

'It's really sad how desperate actresses have become these days; especially as they get older that they'll do anything to get attention!! So LS, I say! hain na?'

LS? Lower Society? Okay now I'm going to have to pound her to pulp . . . Venky and Sam grab my arms before I can begin to unleash my MMA moves, when suddenly, in the middle of their cackles and sniggers, Roberto steps out of his car and enters the school gate. I wave and he nods in acknowledgement. Instantly Nikita's face changes from mean to really vicious. She's gearing up for another spat. I look around anxiously and am relieved to see two of Roberto's soccer pals join him as he starts walking towards us. Maybe that should deter her from doing anything stupid.

The second bell for assembly goes off and students start pouring in, rushing towards their classes; Roberto's a few feet away when Tarantula fires the last salvo knowing that now we'd have to just sit tight until lunch recess to get back at her.

'My Mom says our Indian culture is going to the dogs these days. That thanks to all these western filmy influences around us, we don't respect marriages any more. The minute someone offers you the chance to act in a film, out goes the responsibility towards the family.'

Nikita's got an audience now; students are stopping, sniggering and whispering, pointing at me. Karan's joined

Tarantula, he's got a giant smirk plastered on his face. He knows his evil-incarnate lady love well and adores her anyway. Roberto walks past them towards us, coolly ignoring the duo, his face angry when Karan yells out, baiting him.

'Go home you phirangi, and take your great western culture with you!'

Huge mistake Oberoi . . . That ticks off Roberto's soccer mates, who are walking with him, big time. They charge towards Princi's office to register a complaint against the two bullies. This sets off a delightful chain of events. By afternoon, there are over twenty complaints of bullying against Nikita Vakil (including by yours truly) forcing principal Nalini Ma'am to summon Ramona Vakil immediately, the very same evening!

* * *

Sam's latest hare-brained scheme—to go where no one has gone before and that is—directly into the hedges underneath the open window of Princi's office! I think Sam should seriously think about becoming a spy . . .

'Do we have to do this, Sam? What if we get caught? I need to get home and work on my designs . . . yes I'd love to hear justice delivered, but really, sneaking around like this, again?' Well, we all know that pleading with a pig-headed BF is quite useless so I ultimately resign myself to whatever fate has in store for me!

We pretend to head to the stationary department which is right opposite Princi's window and quickly plant ourselves in the hedges. Sam and I are right under the window, two ears better than one theory while Venky's a little further down where he can spot visitors and alert us on our cell phones.

'RV& NV coming now,' texts Venky; he's squinting through the binoculars, 'Princi's office.'

'All right Angie, keep your head down, don't get too excited and keep very, very quiet!' whispers Sam. Whaaat! I roll my eyes in exasperation.

'*You* need to keep quiet not me!' I hiss when I hear Ramona's voice cut through. I quickly put my finger to my lips warning Sam.

'It is such a pleasure being here. To build a school is one thing but make it grow requires like-minded people who share the same vision. But sadly,' and here Ramona Vakil actually clucked like a hen, 'when the school does not discipline those students who behave like goondas because of their filmi backgrounds, bad things are bound to happen influencing innocent minds, polluting them with thoughts that go against the very grain of our great Indian culture.'

OMG! Praying mantis thinks she's on air.

'Why just yesterday on Starry News Chanel, we were debating Stars and Marriage . . .'

'Yes, I watched that interview, Ms Vakil; your viewpoint is very interesting, but let's keep that conversation for another day. Right now it has been brought to my attention that your daughter Nikita has been instigating and participating in bullying certain students. One of them *being* Kajol Kulkarni's daughter, Geetanjali.'

There is a long, uncomfortable silence. We hold our breaths, wondering what's going to happen next.

'In this particular case she has stolen her sketchbook, verbally abused the child and then deliberately ripped up her prom dress. There are witnesses.' Princi's tone is getting frostier by the minute.

And then Nikita squeals tearfully, 'No ma'am, there's nothing of that sort, really! These two, Geetanjali especially and that Sampurna friend of hers, are always so jealous of me.' And Tarantula bursts into tears.

'You're such a liar Nikki! Ma'am, Nikita and her gang, always pick on me, it's everything, from my mother being an actress, to my clothes to my friends . . . and she's been bullying me for a long time, you can ask anyone.' I burst out angrily. Our covers are blown!

Principal Nalini is not in the least bit amused.

'This is disgraceful! You have put the great name and reputation of this school, my school, at stake by indulging in such immature behaviour! Hiding in the bushes, eavesdropping! What next?'

It's just the four of us in her office; Sam and I stand there nervously shuffling our feet waiting for the axe to fall, Venky's managed to evade arrest. The Vakils on the other hand are as cool as cucumbers, a devil-may-care smirk plastered on their faces.

'Geetanjali Kulkarni and Sampurna Banerjee, you are suspended for a week. Take that time to reflect on your goals, the academic mess you're always in and hopefully you'll come back more focused and do better than being just the school's fashionista and detective. There will be three assignments to complete before you return, get the details from Ms Subramaniam. Any more such snooping incidents and you will both be immediately rusticated.'

'Good luck girls!' Ramona sneers. 'And do give my regards to your mom . . .' she smiles at me.

'Nikita, you assume that because your father is on the board of Royal International you can behave in any manner and I won't take any action?' Princi's voice drops to a whisper. It's deadly and lethal. Ramona Vakil suddenly realizes that probably things aren't going quite the way they should.

'I completely agree with your mother that it is harmful to the school if we allow bad influence especially *bullying* to flourish.' At that the smug look vanishes from Nikita's face. Ramona is so shocked, she's speechless.

'Despite earlier warnings from your class teacher, there has been no improvement in your behaviour. Therefore, as per the school rules I have no recourse but to cancel your admission with immediate effect. Your school leaving certificate will be couriered home to you. Good day, Ms Vakil.'

We all stumble out of Princi's office in utter shock.

We're on the top of the world!

* * *

'That was simply awesome! Did you *see* Tarantula's face when Princi told her she was being expelled?' Sam says for the hundredth time as we hang out at the CCD next to school.

'Serves her right; she had it coming. All those times she's made our lives hell! God I'm sooo happy! I'm definitely having another cold coffee!'

Roberto's joined us post soccer practice. He's dying to know what happened and we're filling him on the details. He's gone very quiet, listening, sipping his lemonade listlessly. I can sense he feels responsible for getting Nikki expelled.

'Don't even think about it Missoni. Those Vakils, however sophisticated and all that, are serious trouble bro, stay away from them. Here have a donut . . .' Venky quips, not bothering to mince his words. Roberto forces a smile and takes the sugar fix, biting into it hungrily.

'Yeah, guess you're right. Nikita would get real nasty every time you would call about Teen Runway . . . . I told her there's nothing between us,' and then he stops suddenly mid-sentence and looks at me with those eyes. 'Is there?' they seem to ask.

I quickly look aside before I give away too much and catch Venky glaring at Roberto while Sam winks at me, grinning wide. Oh boy, my BFs are going to make life really miserable from now!

15

C4N (CIAO FOR NOW)

Nothing ever completely changes.

Roberto and Venky try bunking school to keep us company on the first day of suspension which is the hardest. Princi has however already made sure that respective parents are in the loop so the usual tummy upset or headache excuse is royally ignored and they are bundled off to school to keep themselves out of trouble.

You bet I'm on cloud nine knowing that Roberto wanted to bunk school just to be with me! Things are definitely hotting up between the two of us, what more can I ask for?

'I'll be at CCD at five, don't be late okay?' He's going to bunk his Hindi class so that we can grab a cup of coffee together. It's time to pump up Pharell William's *Happy*, set the mood for the day!

'Pilloo, use this time to work on your designs,' advises Mom during breakfast. 'Don't waste your time thinking about what's happened.' She's so cool and so practical. No wonder she's such a success story. Mom and Sulu have an appointment with Princi tomorrow; they're going to appeal against my suspension.

'I'm going to be late coming home today, have a dubbing at noon then am being interviewed again on *Tea with Trisha*.' Mom gives me a warm smile, 'Wish me luck so that I win the hamper for you!' and she's gone in a cloud of Chanel No 5.

'I'm off to lunch and then the salon. Will be back by five, be good okay?' Sulu rushes off to get her favourite multani-mitti facial. She swears that it keeps her skin youthful.

So right now, I'm all alone, sipping my green tea. That's right, I actually like this weird stuff these days. Cheetos keeps me company curled up against my laptop, purring softly. I pump up my favourite songs and get into the zone with Maroon 5's *Moves like Jagger*.

'In order to be irreplaceable, one must always be different.' I've got Coco Chanel's famous mantra taped on my soft board and I read it religiously every time before I begin a sketch.

'Be original, yourself; gimmicky designs don't always find takers.' Suzanne aunty had warned when I showed her some outlandish designs that were let's just say, really radical.

My mind is buzzing with a thousand ideas that it's really hard to pick the one best concept for my design collection, when the music changes tempo and Karunesh comes on with his sublime *Global Spirit* songs unleashing a world of exotic images in front of me. Time stills and a sense of calmness comes over me. I play his music like ten times over and the hypnotic rhythms are conjuring up a world of languid days gone past, of history and mystery . . . I can see the concept that will bind the three designs together on the runway . . . love and betrayal over the ages portrayed by a stark red and black palette!

I begin sketching furiously.

First the formal look inspired by the British Raj, red Jodhpur pants with a fitted black kurti. Then the casual look inspired by romantic Italy is a black and red plaid short skirt worn with a red or black ganji. For the evening look, I attempt to tweak the timeless Indian chiffon sari; the body of the sari is jet black, sprinkled with tiny red roses. There are no pleats at the waist instead the pleats wrap across the bosom in Grecian style and sit at the shoulder, a long sash that trails on the floor. The back is completely bare and open adorned with a gigantic single necklace.

'Didi guest aiya hain.' Chotu bangs on my door repeatedly, shattering my eardrums and the glorious magical moment I was floating in!

'Who's there!' I yell exasperated. Who's it at this hour? Don't people realize that afternoons are for reading, relaxing, taking a siesta for god's sake, not for running around disturbing folks! This person better have a good reason for . . .

'Didi woh phirangi hain.' Roberto's here! *Seriously?* What's the time? What's happened? Why didn't he call first? Drat it, my phone's dead!

I dump Karunesh, quickly check my avatar in the mirror, apply a touch of gloss, pat down my hair, forget to change my clothes and rush out of my bedroom, jolting Cheetos out of her catnap. Oops! Think she lost one of her nine lives; she's dived underneath my bed, hackles up.

'Ciao Cara, hope I'm not disturbing you, am I? or something?' Roberto stands nervously shuffling his feet.

Noooo, not at all, I've been dying to meet you, my heart yells but thankfully my brain knows better and instead of that corny dialogue, I say. 'Well, I was just working on the roughs for the contest, but come in, please.'

He smiles that devastating smile and my knees melt away. Why didn't I see your call? I would have dressed up a bit!☹!

Chotu of course scowls and reluctantly vanishes into the kitchen to get us some Coke, alerting Laxmibai on the way who then purposely decides to sweep the living room while we're there. We sit awkwardly with our feet all scrunched up against our chins while Laxmibai investigates every dust particle under our chairs with a zeal that would make Holmes snap her up as his next Watson!

'Come on Roberto, let's go to my room, we'll talk there.' I lose it and proceed to scandalize the help by leading the phirang to my bedroom, and shutting the door!

* * *

Besties have a knack of turning up at the wrong times.

And mine are no different than yours. Cell phones have been invented for a reason, right? But no, we must drop in whenever we feel like, never mind calling up in advance or caring for a certain word called 'privacy'.

'So Roberto, what's up huh?' Sam plonks herself next to me while Venky flanks me on the other, shielding me from whatever news Roberto has brought me.

'I, ermmm, came to tell Angie sumthing important.' He coughs and clears his throat. 'I wanted to talk to her kinda alone, you know.' He tries to assert himself but Sam's glare fizzles out his timid request into an inaudible mumble. The tone of his voice sends my heart racing, no not the nice way, but more like when it's not good news.

'Great! Spit it out, there are no secrets between us.' Three pairs of inquisitive eyes and highly curious ears are now zeroed in on Missoni. He catches my eye; there's a tenderness I haven't seen before. My heart lurches; will he bare his soul now, in front of all? He must have sensed my worry and I know that he's changed his mind for when he begins to speak it's Missoni talking, not the Roberto I know.

'Well, the situation in Iraq has worsened and my father's expertise is required there. So the Italian embassy has decided to recall my father to Baghdad. We leave India in two weeks.'

'Whaat! So suddenly! But I need you. The Teen Runway Contest . . . you have to be there for me!'

The earth vanishes from underneath me, my breath is snatched away and I'm Alice in Lost Land, falling, spinning wildly down the deep, dark terrifying hole. This can't be happening!

* * *

It's never a good time to say good bye.

Roberto loves the Chowpatty so we head down there to soak our toes in the warm, muddy waters of the Arabian Sea. It's still early in the evening and the hawkers are taking their time setting up their stalls, so people leave us alone and we sit content in each other's company.

The evening sun enfolds Roberto in its last rays; he looks like Adonis, so handsome and tragic. I listen to his voice as he tells me about his home and his large family back in Italy. I can tell his heart is already homeward bound and this hurts real bad for I want him to say that he wants to stay here longer, that he will miss me.

The clock is ticking. We must leave in an hour, he has to still finish packing. It is time to say those words which otherwise will remain unsaid. Dare I reach out and hold his hand? Dare I hope that we have something special between us?

Instead I lose my nerve and say, 'Hey Missoni, look wish lanterns! Come on let's go make a wish.' I grab his hand, dragging him to his feet and we race across to the wizened old couple's hand cart.

I watch my red wish lantern sail away into the sky, a wind picks up and it flies onwards towards the horizon, till finally it's a tiny red dot, and then it's gone swallowed up by the vastness. But I know it's still flying, bravely winging its way into the skies above.

'I'll see you in Italy Mia Cara.' Roberto holds my hand in his and raises it to his lips, gently kissing my fingertips.

His eyes hold me in their embrace, and I drown in a sea of emotions, struggling to stay afloat, to remain sane.

'Good luck with the designs. They are fantastic; am sure the judges will love your collection. Just believe in yourself, okay?'

I nod and smile. My eyes are clouding over; I mustn't tear up, not now, so I will my voice to steady up and affirm my dreams.

'Yes, of course, your fashionista is going to follow her dreams, come what may. Full on.' I smile and impulsively hug him.

'And so it shall be,' he pulls me closer and we head back to the shore.

16

FOF (FULL ON FASHIONISTA)

It is the final countdown.

The auditorium is packed to the rafters, and upfront are the judges. Sophia Verduce, Karl Lagerfeld (huge surprise!) and Nayantara Singh of *Vogue India*.

I'm the last participant presenting the finalists' showstopper design. My nine competitors are a formidable lot. Some of them have created fabulous ensembles based on radical concepts. Seventeen-year-old Mir Jafar from Hyderabad based his collection on the theme 'Fasting and Feasting'; his showstopper was a multicoloured see-through anaarkali! The audience had gasped at the audacity and then roared into a tumultuous applause . . . For the first time, I have serious doubts that I can win this contest.

'All the best Mia Cara, you'll rock it, I'm sure. Your lines are great, strong and sexy, don't worry so much, okay?'

Roberto had called just before the show started. 'Here's wishing you all the best and that you win.'

Well, I prayed like I've never prayed before, calling upon the entire pantheon of Indian gods and goddesses, visited the neighbourhood mosque, church, gurudwara, chanted the Lotus Sutra day and night, and then burnt the midnight oil to get these three crucial designs ready.

But it's all going to come down to the audience's reaction to the showstopper design, so please, please god, don't let anything go wrong now.

'And I now present our next finalist, Ms Geetanjali Kulkarni from Mumbai.'

I try my best to glide on to the stage, 'Take smaller steps when climbing, place your foot gently, don't thump and please don't eat up your words!' Mom's hundred and one instructions ring in my ear as I bow to the audience and accept the mike.

'Geetanjali, congratulations on making it to the top ten Teen Runway finalists list. Could you tell us about your collection, The Indian Love Story, and the inspiration behind it?'

I smile and take a deep breath. 'Good evening ladies and gentlemen. It's a great honour to be amongst the top ten Teen Runway finalists. My collection, the Indian Love Story, is inspired by the hope of love and the pain of betrayal. I've used two colours, red and black, to depict these very powerful emotions. To quote the famous poet Khalil Gibran, 'When you love someone let them go, For if they return they were always yours. If they don't, they never were.'

I dedicate this collection to my mother whose life has been one of sublime love and heart-breaking betrayal . . .'

I can see Dad, Sam, Venky and Suzanne aunty right up front sitting next to a lady in an African ensemble. They wave out to me and blow kisses. Dad gives me a thumbs up signal. I wave back and quickly go backstage. It's curtain time.

Suzanne aunty's been a great mentor, helping me understand the importance of detailing and finishing. I know I have loads to learn but am hoping that I've done well enough to live my dream.

Mom's deliberately decided not to attend. 'I'm really upset that I'm going to miss this but pilloo I don't want the media saying that you won because of me.'

'Ladies and gentlemen, Geetanjali Kulkarni presents her showstopper from the Indian Love Story!'

The lights dim. I hold my breath. It's now or never. Haunting strains of *Bombay Pure* fills the air; the spotlight slowly illuminates two young children. The boy wearing red jodhpurs and a black kurti, and the girl wearing a red and black plaid short skirt with a black ganji, the formal and casual wear from my collection.

This smart and sneaky trick was Sam's idea, 'Never mind whether you win or not, this way with the child models on stage as part of your show the audience will be intrigued to see the rest of your designs.'

The twins take the ramp, walking, posing, showering rose petals on to the ramp. The audience is intrigued, when the beats pick up pace and the spotlight slowly unveils the showstopper model who rises from below the centre of the stage through a trapdoor in a cloud of smoke . . . Everyone holds their breaths, wondering who it is, and then break into excited applause. For it's none other than my very glamourous grandmother Sulochana Saxena!

And grandma totally rocks the ramp in those five minutes, her silver hair tied up carelessly in a braid with a single rose, ruby red lips, her sexy bare back sensually swishing to flaunt a gigantic metallic necklace! She makes sure my design is viewed from all angles, stopping and posing just at the right moments in front of the photographers and the judges, doing away with the traditional model poker face, blowing kisses and flashing her gorgeous smile at the audience, thoroughly enjoying the moment.

The crowd goes completely WILD!

I can't believe it! Even the judges are on their feet, clapping.

* * *

The ramp's completely empty except for the stunning, petite blonde in a silver sheath.

It's Sophia Verduce, ready to announce the winner.

'Ladies and gentlemen, thank you for your support in making Teen Runway such an amazing success the first time round. We had over ten thousand entries, out of which we had to choose the top ten—definitely not an easy task. And so, I thank each and every one of the top ten India finalists for the effort and dedication they have put in. We liked all your designs, only some more than the others.' Sophia Verduce's heavily-accented voice has silenced the auditorium. 'But in any contest, there can be only one top dog . . .' The silence is deafening. Backstage everyone's on the edge. Some are huddled fervently praying, others simply rigid, expressionless, like me, waiting for the axe to fall.

'The House of Verduce is looking for young fashion designers who have strong concepts, the ability to experiment in a clever manner and most of all a passion for fashion. One may have the skills or the talent but without passion, nothing will come to life.

And today, we are very pleased to announce that . . .' she pauses for that sickening moment of revelation,

'Geetanjali Kulkarni has been selected unanimously as the Teen Runway finalist from India.'

Sam jumps up, screaming wildly while embarrassed-as-hell Venky's trying to get her to shut up! The audience bursts into a tumultuous applause drowning out my excited shriek!

I have WON!

I find myself being ushered on to stage. Sophia smiles and shakes my hand, Karl and Nayantara are also on stage. They congratulate me warmly. Karl gives me a thumbs up sign.

'As the India Teen Runway finalist, Geetanjali has won a month-long internship at the Chanel Studio courtesy Karl Lagerfeld. She has also won a gift hamper from *Vogue India* courtesy Nayantara Singh. And a gift voucher from the House of Verduce courtesy Sophia Verduce.'

My wish has come true.

I have WON! I'm going to Italy!

I instantly WhatsApp Roberto. *Call u later* ☺*!*

Hearts and bouquets of all kinds flood my cell phone.

'Congratulations Mia Cara! . . . See you in Milan. Talk soon, Love. Roberto' is the message that sends my heart soaring into the skies . . .

* * *

I leave for Italy in a week and there are a million things to get done. I must not forget a single detail.

'You've gotta win Teen Runway, so stay focused Angie!' Sam reminds me every hour, terrifying me no end.

'Just be yourself Angie, don't get stressed.' Roberto messages me.

'Don't overdo a concept. Be original. Be yourself,' is Suzanne Singh's sane counsel.

'Presentation is everything. Make sure you don't lose your nerve under pressure.' That's Mom's pearl of wisdom.

'Just go and enjoy yourself. It's not the end of the world.' Sulu gives her sage advice.

'I'm really proud of you Pillo, whatever happens.' Dad speaks gently.

'I'll be praying for you,' says Venky, on his way to Tirupati.

I read and reread the e-mail twenty times, highlighter in hand.

- The six Teen Runway finalists are Ivana Romanov, Russia. Eric Hu, Hong Kong.

```
     Christian Slater, Kenya. Ken Klein, USA.
     Geetanjali Kulkarni, India and Gianni
     Belucci, Italy.
•    The Teen Runway Grand Finale will take
     place in Italy at the House of Verduce.
•    The finalists will have one week to come
     up with three designs and execute all
     of them. The concept will be declared
     on arrival.
•    Contestants will  be provided with
     supplies and tailoring equipment.
•    Please make sure your passports and visas
     are in order. Send us the details asap.
```

Every major event in your life in India calls for the entire household's involvement. And so, a week later, everyone's come to see me off, including Chotu and Laxmibai.

'Sambhalke staying Chota memsahib, okay?' Chotu scowls, royally butchering up the English and Hindi languages and mangling them into a royal khichdi, wagging his finger authoritatively.

Laxmibai joins in, 'Hain, no looking here, there at phirangi chokras, okay bachcha?' and she hands me a packet of laddos before bursting into tears.

Sulu hurriedly shoos the noisy duo off before we attract more attention from the burly policemen at the airport.

'Well BF, all the very best. Go conquer Italy but don't get distracted by certain Italians and do come back home,' Sam gently teases me, while Venky, all shaved from Trupati, gets choked up and gives me a bear hug. 'I'll miss you, Angie.'

'I'll miss you guys too, but I'll be back soon. We'll Skype okay? Where's Mom? And Dad?' I frantically scan the jostling crowds at Mumbai Airport wondering what's happened; I need to check in soon, when I spot Dad hurrying a blonde towards us! What's he doing? Who's that woman? Where's Mom? Before I can quiz him, the strange lady is in front of me and I find myself looking into my mother's eyes!

'Whaat? Mom? Why are you dressed like this?'

'Hi I'm Mata Hari, the famous spy, master of many disguises,' she grins wickedly.

OMG! Mom had been in the audience that night, all the time! Totally ingenious I must say!

'You were amazing, you've done so well! I'm so proud of you!' her eyes shine with joy.

'Aren't you coming with me? Like you said . . .' I'm suddenly apprehensive, never having travelled so far, alone.

'Nope, pilloo, you're on your own. Enjoy the freedom, don't worry, you'll be fine . . .' she smiles and hugs me tightly. 'We've spoken to the airline. It's a non-stop flight and they have arranged an escort for you till Milan. Isabella called me and told me they will be there to pick you up at Milan Airport. You will stay the night with them and then they will drop you to the House of Verduce. Isabella will be your local guardian during your stay. She mentioned Roberto has plans to show you around Rome and Milan, I believe . . .' she smiles cheekily.

'So off you go . . . win or lose, always believe in yourself, my Full On Fashionista!'

* * *

As I wing my way, my eyes fall on a beautiful quote by Khalil Gibran, 'Trust in dreams for in them is the hidden gate to eternity.'

And I know, my dreams will come true.

PSST . . . FULL ON FASHIONISTA SPILLS HER SECRETS!

1. Know Your Body Shape
V necks, empire waists or A lines help slim down the top-heavy Apple body shapes. Dark-coloured skirts or trousers help Pear body shapes look slimmer around the hips. Always draw attention to your best features.

2. Sport It
Exercise regularly to keep fit and in shape.
Makes shopping so much it fun!

3. Go Classic
A white shirt and a pair of denims are a must have.

4. Grab That LBD
No girl's wardrobe is complete without that perfect Little Black Dress.

5. Dare to Bare, with Care

Too Much Skin is not in, so don't go *too* sheer
with the transparent look.

6. Don't Cling Wrap

Avoid fabrics that cling to your body and accentuate your
problem paunch and love handles.

7. Mix n Match

Put together upscale brands and regular street clothes
to create your very own exciting fashion ensembles.

8. Colour Your Wardrobe Bright

Liven up your day with a bright orange scarf, pink jacket
or neon handbag!

9. Check That Line

Cover panty lines in skin-hugging pants. And ensure that
your cleavage is just right.

10. Tight Is Just Tacky

Don't squeeze yourself into undersized clothes making
everything pop out in the wrong places!

11. Go Petite Fleur

Remember that bigger motifs or flowers will always
make you look more than you weigh.

12. Trend with Taste
Don't blindly ape trends; if something doesn't appeal,
just drop it.

13. Salon It
Regular once a month essential grooming makes heads,
and hearts, turn.

14. Bag These
A good quality lip gloss, kohl, deodorant for a quick fix.
Anytime, anywhere.

15. Go Au Natural
Minimal make-up with just a touch of gloss and kohl
keeps your skin clean and clear.

16. Heel It Well
Wear comfy heels no more than 2 ½ inches. Keep the
killer stilts for the occasional runway.

17. Spitz It On
Choose perfumes and deos that make you smell fruity
and fresh all day long.

A SNEAK PEAK INTO
ANGIE'S SKETCHBOOK

Punk Rockstar—with a touch of Goth.

Knee-length dress with ruffles

Not too many.

Dump dark colours for eye popping palette.

Neon green? Orange?

Set off with black fishnet stockings and knee-length combat boots.

Neat!

Kohl eyes, metallic jewellery and scrunchy loose hair?

Perfect!

Prom Dress—with a Greek twist.

Camouflage and lace evening gown,

VIP keep print small!

Fluid lines like Grecian drapes, but short in front with cutaway.

Check length!

Add Peekaboo lace midriff.

Cool!

One off shoulder with flowy sash to the ground.

Love it!

Read More in Puffin

DOA Detective Files: Trouble at the Taj

Sonja Chandrachud

Travel back in time with the DOA gang as they solve out-of-this-world mysteries using their wits, will and Tuk Tuk, their auto rickshaw with attitude, which also happens to be a time machine!

DOA Case File 1 Agra, India, 1636: There's some serious trouble at the Taj! Chief architect of the Taj Mahal, Ustad Ahmed Lahauri, has been kidnapped, leaving work on the construction unfinished. Emperor Shah Jahan now has to find a new architect for his dream project. But the ghost of his dead empress, Mumtaz Mahal, is determined to not let any other architect work on her mausoleum. She summons the DOA detectives and commands them to find the missing architect before its too late and she's saddled with a hideous tomb for eternity.

Soon the detectives discover that there is much more to the Ustad's disappearance than a mere kidnapping. There is a traitor in the imperial court who will stop at nothing till he fulfils his evil designs! Who could it be? Will the detectives be able to stop his wicked plans? Will they be able to ensure that the magnificent Taj Mahal gets built?

Read More in Puffin

DOA Detective Files: The Revenge of the Pharaoh

By Sonja Chandrachud

Travel back in time with the DOA gang as they solve out-of-this-world mysteries using their wits, will and Tuk Tuk, their autorickshaw with attitude, which also happens to be a time machine!

The Sceptre of Ra has been stolen, putting the Horus Throne in danger. Pharaoh Hatsheput must find the regal sceptre before the new moon or give up the throne to her nephew, the young and ambitious pharaoh-in-waiting, Thutmosis III. Desperate, she summons her father, Thutmosis I, from the dead and sends him to bring in the DOA detectives to solve this perplexing mystery before the new moon.

Soon, the detectives discover that there is much more to the theft. An attack by a black cobra, a poisoned drink, ill omens everywhere . . . something sinister is definitely afoot in the great palace. Will the detectives be able to counter Egyptian heka magic and find the sceptre and the thief in time, or will Hatshepsut carry out her threat of throwing them to the crocodiles?